Serpent & Nique: When Love is True

Michelle Kay

December 2015

Frost clouded the windows as I sat across from Serpent, in a booth at this diner called Lover's Lane; a place on Serpent's side of town where couples hung out at. I was stirring my cup of hot chocolate with a candy cane, dressed down comfortably in a pair of Victoria Secret sweats and American Eagle boots on my feet. It was the only thing in my wardrobe that I could squeeze my ass into without feeling like a fat cow. I was craving something sweet when Serpent picked me up from the airport for the holiday break but now that I was back in Houston, I suddenly had a loss of appetite.

"What's wrong with you, Nique?" Serpent inquired with concern was in his voice.

I could feel him staring at me as he moved my mug out of the way and thumbed the whip cream off my lower chin, giving his thumb a taste. I couldn't help but simper as he placed one of his soft kisses onto my full, blush lips. I could swim in Serpent's deep dark waves, Creole red skin, and onyx eyes; forging him to look like a Frenchmen with charms that placed me right under his spell. Serpent and I had been together since our sophomore year of high school. Even when my parents had found out that we were dating and forced me to break up with him, that was the first time I had ever broken the rules. For my parents to both be doctors, they never educated me on sex at all. Maybe they felt like they were protecting me, but it didn't do me any good, being that I ended up finding out how sex worked for myself. Serpent was the only person I had been intimate with and what we couldn't do at school, we would do after school at his mother's house. I didn't like sneaking around my parents, but it was the only way I could be with him.

One day, when I was booed up in Lover's Lane with Serpent, the mocha colored pigments must of flushed from my face when I saw my father storm into the diner dressed in his doctor's coat, looking like Dog The Bounty Hunter, capturing a fugitive on the run. After threatening Serpent to stay away from me or else, my father yanked me up out of the booth, pulling me all the way outside and pushing me into the car where my mother was waiting for me in the backseat. My parents thought I was at school volunteering to tutor my fellow classmates but when my teacher called informing them that I hadn't volunteered in weeks, they drove around the city searching for me. After that incident, they grounded me until I turned eighteen and never trusted me with a piece of freedom again.

When I graduated from high school with honors I thought the accomplishment would be good enough for my parent's to approve of me and Serpent's relationship, but they told me that my education was the only thing important and that the only way I could be successful in life, is if I followed in their footsteps. With no questions asked they sent me away to Harvard so that I could become a doctor and work at my father's hospital. Serpent had told me one day over the phone that college was never in his plans, that he was just thankful that his mama even got the chance to see him walk the stage and accept his high school diploma. He mentioned that he only wanted to get a good paying job and help pay the bills at his mother's house. Serpent and I were still together but the long-distance relationship, was causing a strain. Not because I thought he was cheating, he had never given me a reason to not trust him, but because we were living in two different cities and we were in love. Why did I love him you ask? Because even though we were so many miles away, we promised each other that we would do whatever we had to do to make our relationship work; even if that meant we could only see each other from time to time.

After going the summer without seeing each other, Serpent had requested some time off from his new job, putting money aside to book a plane ticket from Houston to come visit me at the university. He would spend the night with me in my dorm room until Monday, when it was time for me to go to class. Although it wasn't the ideal relationship it was working for us, up until reality had hit me. My period was a month late and when I went to the clinic on campus, I found out that I was six weeks pregnant. I knew I would be making one of the most important decisions that I ever had to make in my life, having to choose between prolife or prochoice. I felt like I was stuck between a rock and a hard place. I wanted to make my parents happy by staying in school, but I also knew in order to do that, I would have to get an abortion and I just couldn't bare the pain of going through that. I was in love with Serpent. How on earth could I abort something that was a part of the both of us? So, four months of being pregnant, there I was. Sitting in a diner clouded by my inner thoughts, with an upset stomach and a fat ass.

"Can you just take me home?" I asked Serpent in my baby voice, not really ready to go home.

If I had it my way, I would have spent the entire holiday break with him but I knew the right thing to do was to put my big girl panties on and have Serpent drop me off at my parent's house. I was biting my nails down to the nubs because my nerves were getting the best of me, and I knew I had to have the talk with my parents.

"Yeah aight; whatever you want, Nique." Serpent nodded

and slipped on his red Texan's leather jacket, before helping me out of my seat.

He blended in with every Houstonian nigga, with a polo white tee underneath his jacket, starched loose fitting jeans with the Black label in the back, and white forces on his feet; he was most definitely from H-town. At 5'5 we both averaged out at the same height. Sometimes I couldn't stand it because people would say we could pass for siblings, but Serpent didn't give a fuck and he proved that every time by showing me public affection whenever he had the chance to.

"Just hold up right quick." He told me as he sprinted over to the candy machine.

When Serpent was done, he opened the door for me, as we headed outside to what felt like walking into an ice box. I was hit in the face with a disrespectful gust of cool air that caused my teeth to chatter. I knew it was from the season of winter that was slowly invading the city. As the dead leaves rustled loudly in the wind, the unpredictable cold weather caused Serpent to blow his warm breath into the ball of my hand.

"You know I love you right?" he told me as we strolled down the icy sidewalk together.

"I love you too." I told him back before he stopped me in the middle of a busy crowd. It was so cold, that I could see a clouded fog form in front of my mouth.

"Serpent why are we," I froze in place as he went into the depth of his pocket, taking out a plastic capsule, where a pink heart shaped ring sat inside.

"I know this isn't like every girl's best friend because it isn't a diamond ring but one day, I promise it will be." He said in seriousness, as he rubbed the baby phat of my stomach before getting onto one knee. "Nique, you've been holding me down since we were in high school and I can't see myself being with nobody else but you."

I was smiling because Serpent had a way of making me feel like I mattered; like I was important in his world. As I moved the piece of long hair that was sticking to my Burt's Bees waxed lips, I listened to Serpent spill his soul out to me.

"I remember the first time I seen your fine ass in high school, you were sitting at a desk in the front row, with your glasses on. While the other girls were grouped up, gossiping about the boys, you had your legs crossed and was all into your schoolwork. I was the new kid coming in the middle of the school year. When the teacher pulled me into the classroom introducing me in front of the class, I remember she made me sit behind you because that was the last empty seat left. Damn was I glad to be seated behind you," Serpent expressed.

"When I found the courage to tap you on your shoulder and ask you for your name, you turned around and rolled your eyes at me before tending back to your work. You were a geek at the time, but that shit was so fuckin sexy to me. I thought you was mean because I had never seen you smile but I ain't even much give a fuck about that; if anything, that made me wanna talk to you even more. That's when I came to school the next day, wrote my number down and placed the note into your lap, right before the school bell rung." he smirked proudly as he licked his pink cushioned lips, revealing a mouth full of straight teeth. I giggled at his remark.

"I low key thought you was just gone throw it away. Your fine ass surprised the shit out of me when you called me that night. Even after your strict ass parents wanted you to break up with me, I knew when you cried in my arms about it behind the back of the schoolhouse, that I couldn't just let you go."

My hands were cupped over the bridge of my nose, as I tried to cover the tears that swelled into my eyes. I listened to Serpent continue to express his feelings to me.

"Even though you won't admit it because you're trying to stay strong for us, I know you super bombed about putting college on hold, but Nique I want you to know that I would never want me or our baby to get in the way of you pursuing your dreams. This ring here, is my promise to one day give you the dream wedding that you deserve. After you have the baby and finish getting your degree, I promise I'ma marry you, girl; I'm in it to win it all the way. Question is, is you in it to win it with me?" Serpent asked as his brown eyes of liquid surveyed me.

By this time, a crowd of pedestrians had formed a circle around us, and everybody was waiting on an answer from me.

"Baby, you know I am." I sniffled as he pushed the promise ring up my finger. "I love you so much, Serpent." I couldn't keep my excitement in as I jumped into his arms, kissing him repeatedly.

To others, the ring might have just been a piece of cheap plastic, only worth a quarter out of the candy machine, but I didn't even much care about that because it was special, and it belonged to me. Serpent was my only support system. He was also the only one that knew I was four months pregnant. Even though he was mad because I made him keep the news from his mama, he respected the fact that I wanted to tell my parent's first before I told anybody else. I couldn't even believe that I held the secret in for as, long as I had but that was just the icing on the cake. I had decided to take the rest of the semester off and I knew my parents were going to freak when they find out that their goody two shoes, honor roll, bookworm student, had failed at completing the one thing they expected me to finish.

When Serpent dropped me off at my parent's house, it only took my mother one second to look at the small pudge that formed in the middle of my stomach to confirm that the dream she had with fishes was about me.

"I knew it! You stupid little girl!" My mother said in a rude tone. "We raised you to be so much smarter than that! What do you know about love? What do you know about raising a baby, when you're still a baby yourself?"

"I know enough to know that Serpent and I love each other." I said with folded arms. "And I'm not a baby anymore, mother, I'm grown!"

I can't even look at you right now!" She said before sending me straight to my father's home office, making me confess every little intimate detail.

"Father I'm four months pregnant by Serpent and I dropped out of medical school this semester to have my baby." I told him while facing his back, as he sat in his office chair while typing on the keyboard in front of his computer. "But father I swear everything is going to work out because Serpent and I will be getting married in the future, when I graduate college and we've made a promise to be together as a family."

My father turned away from his studies, taking his reading glasses off to fully focus his attention on me.

"Your mother and I try to provide you with the best life we can; even sending you off to one of the best colleges in the country on a full ride, so that you can make something of yourself and this is how you repay us?" He asked without even giving me time to respond. "If having a baby is that easy, don't you think your mother and I would have had more kids? We damn near sacrificed having you! Your mother was pregnant with you when we both were attending medical school and although she wanted to give up on her studies and drop out of school to solely focus on you, I wouldn't let her. But you are grown now and since it sounds like your mind is already made up, I see no reason for me to try to change it."

"So, what are you saying?" My mother came from behind me and asked my father.

"I'm saying that I didn't raise a daughter to dishonor us by dropping out of college to have a baby under our roof. And since she was grown enough to lay down and make a baby, well then she's grown enough to raise the baby on her own."

"But husband,"

"But nothing! MY WORD IS FINAL!" My father shouted as he cut his eyes at my mother, who ran down the stairs and cried.

In that moment, her and I both knew that it was no talking my father out of that one. I stood in the doorway of my father's office with enough shame to trace my eyes down towards the floor.

I didn't gaze back at my father until he stepped in front of me and said, "From this day forward, I want you out of this house." He instructed in a serious tone. "Don't even think about leaving with anything that's in this house, you no longer need our help, that's what you have a fiancé for. You will not come back to this house asking your mother and I for financial help, or any type of help for that matter. As far as we know it, you're a disgrace to this family and I don't want to see your face anymore."

My father's words felt like they'd cut an open wound through my heart. As my mother cried at the kitchen table, my father showed me to the door with a quickness; only saying that he and my mother loved me, but it was for my own good. It didn't really hit me that I no longer had my parents support, until I jumped from my father slamming the door, turning the top lock.

I stood outside in the rain and caught the bus all the way to Serpent's mother's house. That was the first time I cried on Serpent's pillow. It was the first time I realized that I was alone and that all I had was him. I was so upset that I went into early contractions that night, that had me feeling like I was about to die. Serpent was by my side the entire time as I went into labor, but before I could even hold my baby, nurses rushed him to the NICU. That's when I heard doctors talking outside of my room, saying that it was an 80 percent chance that my baby wouldn't make it to live through the night and if he did survive, he would surely develop a disability with a long list of medical issues. All I could do was say a prayer to God because he was the only one who could turn the situation around. Screw the doctor's medical knowledge because my baby was a miracle baby.

When Serpent rolled me to his incubator, my baby was hooked up to all different types of cords; including having to be fed through a feeding tube, while depending on an air ventilator. Granted I knew the moment I witnessed my miracle baby grip his daddy's pinkie with his tiny little finger, I had the greatest gift that I could ever ask for. I had my family.

Five Years Later

"Good night, Mommy." Zion said, as he climbed into his twin-sized bed with his Ninja Turtle figurine and matching slippers.

My baby was the spitting image of his daddy, with both of our personalities intertwine and I absolutely adored him.

"Good night, Zion." I cooed as I gave him a peck on his cheek.

I began tucking him snug on each side, shaking my head as his eye lids grew heavy. He was the type of child who tried to fight his sleep until the very end, but of course sleep would always win. I pulled the switch down to his night light, cracking the door halfway closed, where I could still see his face. I smiled as I looked at him one last time before walking downstairs hoping to do some speed cleaning, prior to getting in the bed to study.

I had made the decision to get back into school whenever Zion was old enough to be enrolled in school himself. Since my parents were no longer helping me pay for school, I had to take out a bunch of student loans and Serpent had been helping me by paying the loans off in return. I'd ditched studying to become a doctor and was attending my last year in ultrasound school. I was only a semester away from becoming a prenatal ultrasound technician but being a mother and a fulltime student, was one of the hardest things I had ever tried to accomplish. If it wasn't for me having my son right when I did, I don't think I would've been motivated enough to keep dealing with the headache of school. Zion was the one pushing me through it. Without him, I don't think I would've even made it this far.

"Dammit!" I shouted, while hopping the rest of the way down to the bottom of the staircase, picking up one of Zion's Lego's that stabbed me through the arch of my foot. You didn't know pain until you stepped on one of them small pieces of fuckers.

I was ready to hit the sheets in an ivory tank and boy shorts; all I needed was for Serpent to come home so I could lay in his arms while I studied. I went into the dining room where I was helping Zion with his math homework, picking up his folder and searching around the house for his backpack. Good thing I had ordered pizza for dinner because I damn sure didn't feel like cooking. Most nights Zion and I ate without Serpent because he worked twelve hours shifts down at the oil plant. We didn't even celebrate Christmas with him last year because he had to go to work. After Zion turned six weeks old, we moved out of his mother's house. Since his mother was handicap, we settled into some two-bedroom apartments around the corner from her house. It wasn't the best, looking apartments but it worked for our household of three.

I strolled into the kitchen placing Zion's folder into his backpack before washing a few dishes left over in the sink. I could hear, the sound of keys jingling in the door right before Serpent walked in, clunking his work boots into the kitchen. Even after a long day of work, my baby daddy looked good in his red chemical jumpsuit and white hard hat.

"These are for you Queen," He stated, handing me a bouquet of roses that was hidden behind his back before placing his hands under the running water and using the dish washing liquid to scrub the grime off of his skin.

"Thank you, baby." I told him as my tongue found its way in his mouth.

Even after years of being together, he still made me feel like that little schoolgirl. I took out a vase from the top cabinet, filled it halfway with water, stacked the flowers in the vase and centered the glass on the island counter. Serpent worked hard for our family and he knew it didn't take a lot to make me happy. I would choose a date that involved my Hulu account, over dining at some fancy restaurant any day.

"You know you're always welcome." He whispered while coming up behind me, to grip me around my waist. Serpent's dick was hard as steel between my cheeks.

"Ohhhhh," I let out a soft moan.

Dropping my head back, I lightly kissed him on the inside of his neck. Serpent's cold hands slid up my tank; he began pinching my nipples with his wet fingers. If he'd checked the seat of my panties, he would've surely felt my cream. I could feel my headlights turn on, as my buttoned, chocolate, areola's peeked through the sheer of my shirt.

"As bad as I wanna fuck you on this counter right now, I planned for us to go out tonight." Serpent grinned.

"Serpent why are you now just telling me this?" I turned around and ask. "You know I just put Zion to bed, I gotta get up in the morning to take him to school before my eight o'clock class. Not to mention that I still have to study." I said as he followed behind me up the stairs.

"I know, I know," He said, as if he had been preparing for my speech. "That's why I asked my mother if she can come over here and watch Zion for the night." Serpent noted, while taking off his work clothes and throwing them into the hamper.

"But Serpent, you know I don't like bothering your mama." I told him as I sat down at my vanity in our bedroom, undoing my ponytail while running my fingers through my hair.

It wasn't that I didn't like his mother, I loved her; I just never liked asking her to watch Zion because she had already done so much. She was like a second mother to me, being that I couldn't talk to my own.

"Don't worry about all that," Serpent tried to reassure me. "Besides, it's too late to cancel plans because my mama already on her way now."

When I didn't look too thrilled, I could sense some agitation as he changed the tone up in his voice.

"Damn, Nique! Ain't I'm the nigga who just got off work? I mean come on! You act like you the one who worked a twelve-hour shift on the plant. Stop overthinking for once in your life and just go out with me," He begged.

Nude as day, he stood in front me while swinging his two-toned, circumcised dick in my face. Serpent had sometimes failed to realize that although I didn't put a pair of boots on and work seven days a week like he did, being a fulltime mother and student was just as much as a fulltime job to me. That was why I couldn't wait to finish school and become an ultrasound tech, so that Serpent didn't have to work so many hours at the plant, and we could spend more time as a family.

"Alright, daddy." I stood up, forcing a half smile on my face.

"Good girl. Now go put you on some makeup and get into something nice; like that dress I bought you that you never wore." He told me as he smacked me on my ass before sending me on my way.

Serpent McKinney

I knew Zonnique was somebody I wanted to be with the day I saw her give birth to my son, Zion McKinney. That was the first day a nigga had ever shed a couple of tears and it was also the day I became a man. Zonnique was the type of woman you'd want to provide a life of royalty to. Yeah, I could have went to college to get a degree and became one of them professionals with a fancy suit and tie, but I wasn't about to leave my mama because I was all she fuckin had. That's the reason I fell in love with Nique because she understood that, and she loved me when I didn't have shit to my name. Don't get it fucked up, life wasn't always a struggle for my mother and, I. She was happy before she had a stroke, that left the right side of her body paralyzed.

Mama used to say she knew I had a fascination with snakes before I even came out the womb. She used to tell me about the story when she was nine months pregnant, saying she didn't have a clue what my name was going to be until her and my grandmother took a camping trip down by this bayou in South Texas. She'd tell me about the night she was sleeping in her tent; she woke up to a piercing sharp pain on the side of her stomach. She'd realized that she'd been bitten by a poisonous snake, whose venom was supposed to kill us both. As she was taken to the hospital, most people would've been in agonizing pain, with their skin decaying right off the bone, but mama said she only felt this euro-phobic high. Doctors then performed an emergency c-section on her, not knowing if I would be dead or alive. She said, she remembered how the anesthetic did nothing for her as she laid still on the cold table, while feeling every cut and incision. When they finally pulled me out of her stomach, holding me over the blue, surgery covering sheet, she knew then my name was destined to be Serpent.

I was a teen when my mother married my stepfather, Cyrus, the richest owner of oil in Houston Texas. She used to describe herself as the black Cinderella, who'd finally found her prince. Mama met Cyrus, back when it was just us and she was working a part time job as a housekeeper, cleaning the inside of mansions that were owned by black people living like they were in the Hampton's. She would always tell me the story about when she was on her hands and knees, scrubbing the floor inside of the biggest house she'd ever seen. That was when Cyrus walked up to her. Mama said he made her drop the bristle brush back into the bucket of dirty water and told her that she would never have to clean up a house again, because she'd be living in one with him. Too bad her fairy-tale story didn't last. Till this day, all I remember is me and my mama coming back one night from one of our summer trips.

I was still in the car when she went in the house to tell Cyrus we were back home. I don't know what happened inside of the mansion, but mama didn't look too, happy when she came back out of the house. She was red in the face and was crying, holding on to her chest like it hurt. All she said was that we were going to my grandmother's house and that we no longer lived in the castle. That night, I overheard mama in the kitchen; she was crying because she caught Cyrus having sex with a younger woman in a bed inside of the house. Guess it was some young tramp Cyrus and mother had agreed to take in because she needed a place to stay.

After my mother got a separation from Cyrus, the dirty rich bastard was quick to throw all, of our things out on the streets. We ended up having to move back into the hood, in the same section eight housing apartments my mother first raised me in. I even transferred from schools; we'd literally went from riches to rags.

The only thing that was good in my life, was Zonnique. Mama was happy that I found love, but I could tell she was depressed. She wasn't as happy as she used to be, and it was showing. Her hair became frail and gray, she wasn't as upbeat as she used to be. It wasn't long after that when she had the stroke. Doctor's claimed it was because of stress, but I knew it was from a broken heart. That was when I got hooked up with a job at Cyrus's refinery and told my mama that she would never have to lift a finger ever again.

After I finished taking a shower and getting myself together, I was stepping out of the bathroom when I heard the doorbell ring. Since Zonnique was sitting at her vanity doing her hair and makeup, I went downstairs and opened the front door to see my Mama, Joyce, standing in the doorway with an overnight bag on her shoulder.

"Come here and give your mama some sugar, son. You look nice' Serpent!" She complimented. "Now where's my grand baby at?"

I gave her a kiss and a hug before helping her with her bag. As she limped inside with her cane, we both walked into the living room.

"Shidddd, Sleep." I told her as I plopped down on the sofa while she sat next to me, putting her feet up on the ottoman.

"Preciate you watching Zion for us while we go out tonight, Mama. I know it was kind of last minute for you to have to get out of the house and come over here."

When I reached into my wallet to chunk her a hundred, dollar bill, of course she wouldn't accept. So, I dropped it inside of her purse when she wasn't looking.

"Oh, hush up." She shooed. "You know I hate when you say the word watch. You and Zonnique both, know I'm always down to spend some time with my grandbaby. Shoot-I don't see Zion enough! You know kids grow an inch taller everyday now; how has everything been going with you and your boss at the job?" She asked referring to her husband and my stepfather Cyrus.

"Work is work," I hissed. "You know me, and boss don't have much to say to each other when I'm up there."

She then shrugged. "I don't want you to still be holding a grudge against him because of something that couldn't work out between me and him when you were a teen. Even though we decided to separate, I hate that you and your stepbrother, True, have lost contact with one another; Lord knows y'all relationship suffered the most. But son, despite how me and him ended things, you have to learn to learn how to forgive and move on."

I listened to my mother ramble while surfing through channels, stopping at the sports channel where a college pregame was in the third quarter. I was watching the game for at least an hour, before I was about to fall asleep.

"Serpent, I'm dressed." Zonnique called out from the top of the staircase.

No longer focused on the game, I took my eyes off of the television, standing up to see my beauty queen as she slowly walked down the staircase. My Queen was looking like she'd came straight out of an Ebony Magazine. She was the color of deep roasted pecans, fine as wine in a thigh, high velvet dress that hugged her hourglass figure nicely. The texture of her jet-black hair was long and wavy, with one side swooped behind her ear; where you could see the flash of the gold hooped earring that I'd gotten her for Christmas, with the cursive word *Nique,* custom made inside. She favored a dark-skinned Cuban Doll, with almond shaped, champagne colored eyes and naturally long lashes.

"Fuck, Zonnique." I whispered.

I pulled her close to me trying to grasp all, of her ass in the palms of my hands, forgetting all about my mama sitting in the living room. I carefully sucked on Nique's big bottom lip; no doubt, this girl had my nose wide open.

"Ya'll two love birds stay here any longer, I don't think you two will even make it out of the house," Mama Joyce called out from the couch.

"Thank you for staying over, Joyce." Zonnique blushed, giving my mama a hug before we got into the car.

When we arrived at Lover's Lane, I left my phone in the car before walking inside with Zonnique on my arm. I knew she would rather be back at home in the books, but it felt good to show her off, and I wanted to do something special for her. As the hostess walked us to a table, every nigga in the spot forgot about the girl they came with. Zonnique looked uncomfortable from all, of the stares but trust and believe I didn't. I used that moment to smack her juicy ass before she sat down in the booth.

"What will you two love birds be eating for tonight?" The waitress said as she pulled out a pencil and note pad to jot down my order.

"The regular." I replied. She scribbled down the order before walking away.

"Baby, if I would have known we were coming in here," Zonnique muttered. "I would of chose to wear something else. I feel overdressed compared to everybody else." She said trying to pull her mink coat over her breast.

"Chill, Nique." I told her. "Me and every other nigga in here, think you look fine as fuck."

When she laughed and snorted, it reminded me of when she used to be a nerd back in high school. I thought it was cute the way she always tried to hide her smile.

Babe can you believe I'm bout to graduate from ultra-sound, school?" Zonnique asked me cheerfully. "I wonder if my parents were to see me now, do you think they would even be proud of me?"

"Of course, they would, Nique. And if they don't then fuck em." I responded, hoping the subject of her parents wouldn't put a damper on our night. "You did what they thought you couldn't do and that was to enroll back in college after you had our baby boy, Zion." She nodded but I could tell by her gesture that she wasn't so sure.

Zonnique's rich parents could kiss my ass; Especially after her proper talking ass father threatened to shoot me if he were to ever see me touching his daughter again.

Nique and I was caked up when he walked in looking like G.I Joe, in a white doctor's coat. I wanted to slap the shit out of him when he dragged Nique out of the booth, like she'd stole something. Guess that was her mama waiting on her inside of the car. Her father threw her into a tinted all black SUV and scurried off, while I was outside standing there like I got stood up on a date. I would never forget how sad she looked when she told me that her parents wouldn't allow us to be together. Her mother and father had almost broken us up, and that's why I never cared for her people anyway. I mean, how the fuck could you disown your daughter when she was pregnant and needed you the most?

That was why I wanted to give my queen a life she deserved. Now that it was the holidays, I wanted to give my baby her gift early. The server, who looked like she was from out of the eighties wearing a curly side ponytail and a short skirt, rolled on her skates towards our table, balancing a round tray on her shoulder, as she placed Zonnique's order that I surprised her with on the table. A mug of hot chocolate whipped in cream, topped with chocolate chip shavings and served with a candy cane; It was Zonnique's favorite dessert on the menu.

"Awwww, babe. This brings me back to when were teenagers. Is that why you invited me out tonight? To remind me of where we first fell in love?" Zonnique asked as she sucked on the candy cane, before slowly drinking the cup of hot chocolate.

"No, Nique. That's not why I invited you out tonight. I brought you here cause I wanted to remind you why I fell in love with you, and what I had promised you from before." I told her as I took out a teal Tiffany & Co box from my pants pocket.

Opening it, a square mixed cut diamond ring sparkled inside. Now that Zonnique was about to finish school, I was ready to make her my wife.

"Ahhhhhh!" Zonnique squealed while taking a hold of the box, as she began to cry; looking at the ring in disbelief, before beaming her eyes back at me. "Really baby? Are you for real right now?! Is this real, Serpent?"

"It don't get no realer than this," I said as I held out her hand like I did years ago, when I gave her that cheap ass promise ring.

"This is why I wanted to surprise you and ask you, for real-for real this time. Zonnique Ari Jones, I'm going to spoil you with millions. Till then Queen, will you marry me?"

"Yes!" She said as she cried.

After Zonnique accepted my proposal, we finished dining out at Lover's Lane and headed back home on the dark empty streets. As my cell phone began to light up from an incoming call, I gazed down at the screen, cutting off the ringer in time for Nique not to notice. I could look at her and tell that she was sleepy because she was in the passenger seat bundled up in her mink coat, already dozing off before we even made it to the red light. When the light switched to green, I placed one hand on the steering wheel, lightly nudging Zonnique to wake her up as I drove inside of our apartments.

"Huh," She blinked her eyes a couple of times, still delirious from the short nap.

"Damn, I almost forgot. I need to run to the gas station and try to fill up cause I damn sure ain't gon feel like doing it in the morning." I said while placing the gear shift into reverse, about to back up out of our reserved parking space.

"Well just drop me off, then you can go; I'm ready to lay down." Zonnique replied as she loudly yawned.

I knew she was a heavy sleeper and once she laid down, she wouldn't be getting up no time soon. When she undid her seat belt, I reached over to give her a kiss and dropped her off, making sure she got inside of the house before I exited out of the apartment's gate.

Thirty minutes later, I made it to the Chevron gas station. Filling up a tank full of gas, I checked the time to see that the night was still young. I pulled up to a five-star hotel because I knew Nique was in bed, so it gave me just enough time to gamble. I handed my keys over to the valet and walked inside, passing the sliding glass doors, making my way downstairs to this game room where I found a machine with an empty chair. The room was full of people and smelled like money. If it wasn't for the last few games that I had been winning, I wouldn't have been able to buy Nique that diamond ring. I had fell in love with the art of winning a game by chance; all I had to do was spin the reel and match the symbols up across the line.

I played the slot machine for an hour before my cell phone began to go off from a text message. Done with playing on the machine, I took the stairs up to the lobby of the hotel, catching the elevator up to the twentieth floor. I walked down the hallway before finding the door of the presidential suite. I slid the key card to the door of the presidential suite. When it gave me access to go in, Mercedez appeared from out of the living room of the exclusive suite. She was butt naked, while holding a clear bottle of Patron.

"I know you seen me calling and texting you. What took you so long to get here? Huh?" She asked before falling onto the plush hotel's bed. "Oh, let me take a guess; You had to make sure your family was taken care of at home?"

"Don't worry about all of that." I told her as I stepped out of my clothes and grabbed ahold of my aching dick. I stroked my shaft in front of her face and she ran her tongue across delicate her lips, like my dick was a snack. "You been blowing up my phone all day and I'm here now, so what's up?" I challenged.

She was the one who was calling me while I was in the car with Nique and texting me downstairs in the game room. She smiled before taking the bottle of Patron to the head, then crawling on all fours to the edge of the bed. I took the bottle from her and took a swig of the clear burning liquid. Only taking a shot and placing it on the floor because I still had to drive myself home. As she engulfed the length of my dick, my fat thumb found the inside of her bleached booty hole.

"Stick your finger in my hole; just like that, Serpent." She took my dick out of her mouth and moaned, as I jammed my thumb deeper up her anus.

"You like it just like that; don't you girl? Just keep sucking that dick, just like that." I smirked because I knew her pussy was already wet.

I loved Zonnique, but after she gave birth to Zion, she wasn't sexually spontaneous like she used to be, and I was still a man at the end of the day. Nique was always complaining about being too tired to do things and over the years, our sex life had gotten boring. I still wanted to be with her at the end of the day, I wouldn't have proposed to her if I didn't. She was the mother of my child and had always stayed loyal to me, but just like any other nigga, I wanted to have my cake and eat my ice cream too.

Now Mercedez on the other hand was a wild card. I had known of her from my old high school. We had been fucking for quite some time. Just last year, I had spent the holidays with her in a room when Nique thought I was at work. The reason Mercedez and I had been fucking for so long was because the nasty things that I did with her were the things that Zonnique was never willing to do. But if I had to be honest, the only reason I was fucking Mercedez in the first place, was because I wanted to find out everything about my stepbrother, True.

I didn't even know she was in a relationship with True; not until I saw her modeling on this runway at one of the spots I was gambling at. I thought it was meant for me to walk up to her and introduce myself. I didn't even think she would remember me, but I was surprised that she did. We ended up ordering drinks at the bar, then that led to us to checking into a room. We began doing that routine on the daily. We got so close she would tell me all the problems she had in her life and things that she didn't feel comfortable sharing with True. One night when she got drunk and was singing like a canary, she told me that Cyrus would be retiring soon because he was up in age and ready to retire. True would take over his million-dollar empire and as for me, I wanted a slice of the million-dollar pie. If I played my cards right, eventually I'd be able to take a bite.

I turned Mercedez over onto the flat of her stomach, placing the palms of my hands in the arch of her back, spreading her apple bottomed cheeks open. I stroked my penis inside of her cave, gripping a handful of her hair around my wrist. When she threw her pussy back, I could see the moisture of her wetness submerged on the skin of my dick. Before I could even get into it, Mercedez pushed me off, of her, jumping off the bed and scurrying off into the hotel's bathroom suite. I could hear throwing up and my mood had instantly changed. I got back into my clothes because once I heard her sobbing, I knew that she had too much to drink.

As much as I was ready to leave her in the hotel room alone, I needed to make sure that she didn't do nothing crazy before I left. I went into the bathroom and grabbed a washcloth to clean my nuts. When I was done, I picked up one of the plastic cups that was on top of the mini fridge, turning the faucet on to fill the cup with tap water and passing the cup to Mercedez.

"Drink this before I go. I hope you got this room for the night cause your ass too drunk to drive home." I told her as I handed her the cup of water.

"Can I tell you something, Serpent?" She asked me while taking her elbows off the seat of the toilet, still sitting on the marble floor. With blood shot eyes, she wiped the residue of her throw up from off of her lips, before gurgling down the cup of water.

"What's up?" I questioned still leaning with my back against the counter.

"Your stepfather isn't so innocent like everyone thinks he is," Mercedez slurred drunkenly, slumping over as if she was going to melt into the floor.

"What you mean?" I asked her, wanting her to clarify because maybe she was just drunk talking.

"He's into young women." She sniffled. "My cousin sold me to Cyrus when I was just a teen; I signed a contract and everything."

"How you get away with some shit like that and you and True stay together?" I quizzed.

"We fuck in the office of his facility; he even has a sex

room. He told me if I was to ever tell anybody, he'll make sure I won't ever be able to tell anybody because he would make sure that I was dead."

"I need to go; I said too much." She said as she brushed her way pass me.

I took a step back because I figured that she was just bluffing, but the way she got up and ran out of the restroom had told me that she was telling me the truth. Wanting to investigate a little bit more, I chased after her.

"Mercedez, where you goin, ma? Slow down." I said, following behind her as she changed back into her clothes while scrambling for the rest of her things, like she had somewhere else to be.

"Forget that I even said that, I swear to you I'm just drunk." She lied. "You have to promise me that you won't tell anybody. If that secret gets out, I know it only came from you." She said like she was afraid for her life. "I have to go, Serpent. Where are my keys?" She asked as I held her keys hostage around my back.

"You ain't going nowhere, and why the fuck you rushing all of sudden?" I asked her as she could hear the jangle of her keys, realizing that she had just found them. "Give me my keys Serpent!" She said trying to fight me.

"What you just told me, is it true?" I asked while waving her keys in the air.

"It's True." She said before snatching the keys out of my hands and running out of the presidential suite.

True Legend Blackwell

Being the king of kings, I was taught to never be disloyal towards my father and to never bring disloyalty to the Blackwell's name. By the age of eighteen, I had graduated from college and was working as a board member for the financial committee of the biggest oil and energy company on the coast. I woke up at six o' clock sharp every morning because as the saying goes, only the early bird catches the worm. I took my arm from up under my fiancé and stamped my fingers down on my alarm, snoozing the radio a minute early. I got up to stretch, sliding my feet into the Versace slippers in front of my Emperor size bed. I trailed down the grand pillared hallway and into the master bathroom suite, lifting the gold seat to the porcelain. I took a whiz before the toilet automatically flushed itself.

After I got myself together, I changed into a navy, black, Desmond Merrion tailored suit, black tie and gold tie clip; complimented with a Calibre De Cartier rolex, and a pair of swayed Italian loafers on my feet. As I walk back into the bedroom, I searched for my phone that was dinging somewhere in the tangled, silk sheets. When I found it and sat back down on the bed, I turned the screen on scrunching my brows at the number of notifications I'd received on my Facebook app. I didn't even like social media, but I made a profile for my business account. My profile picture was a picture of the oil brand.

When I tapped my finger on the face book app, it logged me into my page. I clicked on the video that my associates tagged me in. As the video played, I was appalled to see Mercedez's face plastered all over the screen. Someone leaked the video of her arrest from the previous night. She was speeding on the streets when a cop turned his lights on behind her. She kept speeding, eventually, making too soon of a turn into a parking lot; jumping the curb and smashing the front hood of her pink Barbie Jeep into a ditch, right before officers helped her out of the vehicle, giving her a sobriety test that she'd fail with flying colors. She was hauled off and booked in the county jail.

Exiting out of the video, I placed my phone down. It was just another thing for the tabloids to talk about. I was a much private person, but somebody was always digging up dirt on Mercedez, trying to tarnish her name. Not that I cared about what people had to say, it only made me mad because people didn't really know Mercedez to make judgments about her. They didn't know her like I knew her.

I was still trying to forget about what could have happened to her when she called me from the inside of the county. I was mad that I had to leave the office early, but more upset that she could of gotten herself killed. Regardless, she was my fiancé and I needed to bail her out. She claimed she'd had too much to drink at the open bar and after she was leaving her modeling gig with her friends at the Marriott hotel, police had turned their lights on, arresting her for another DUI. When I picked her up from the county, she was still drunk out of her mind and I didn't want to talk to her while she was like that. I actually wanted to give her a chance to talk to me about what happened because I hated jumping to conclusions, but I knew she was still too fucked up to talk and I wasn't going to press her about it. Not until she sobered up anyway.

When I asked about the whereabouts of her car, she never told me she wrecked it. She only said that police officers had it towed at the scene because she couldn't get in touch with nobody to drive it home. It sounded like a lie to me but whatever; I wanted to believe her at the time. Nevertheless, I was going to let her sober up and talk to me when the sun came up.

Now that it was thirty minutes to seven, I figured she'd had plenty of time to get some rest. I was trying to wake her up to talk to me before I left for work.

"Mercedez, wake up." I told her while slowly lifting the Egyptian comforter from over her body.

She was yellow boned with a red complexion. Tall in height, she had lean legs, a petite frame, small pointy nose, medium size lips with dotted brown freckles under her oval shaped, olive colored eyes. She was always pretty to me but hearing it so many times before, she didn't believe it anymore. Even when I still tried telling her that she was. Mercedez was laying on her other side when she turned over towards me and balled her body into a fetal position. She shivered. Her ginger colored, red, hair was all poofy and wild like, covering the front of her face. I sat closer to her, moving her hair out of the way to see if that would get her to wake up.

"Not right now, Truuuu," Mercedez mumbled while pushing me away. "Can't you see I'm trying to get some rest after sleeping in that cell with all of them dirty people?" She whined as she began feeling around for the duvet comforter, that wasn't even on the bed. "And give me back the cover because the air is fuckin cold up in here!"

I dragged my hand across my face because Mercedez was stubborn. When she didn't get her way, sometimes she could be immature and outright spoiled; this was the woman I was engaged to. Please don't mistake it, I loved her. I wouldn't have been with her if I didn't, but damn! For Mercedez to have been only a couple years younger than me, she had a lot of growing up to do. Throughout the years I supported her dreams of trying to get signed as a super model; flying her out to runway shows, being there at her model showcases whenever I could make it. Anything I needed to do to help get her discovered, because I believed in her and I knew she could make it.

I scooted closer to her and moved her hair out of her face. I knew she would give me a hard time about disturbing her while she was sleeping, still I needed to see her eyes because that was the only way I knew if she was listening to me or not.

"You wouldn't have had to sleep in a cell if you would have just called the driver and had him take your drunk ass home. You done had enough time to sober up, why you ain't tell me you wrecked your car when you got arrested? You supposed to be my fiancé and you keeping things away from me now?"

"See True, that's why I didn't wanna tell you. I know I'm supposed to be your fiancé; last time I checked I was." She snapped. "Why do you always have to take it there? I knew you would be trippin' with me and going on and on, about how you just got my jeep fixed last month, and how I needed to drink more responsibly when I'm hanging out with my friends. The reason I didn't tell you about the damages on my jeep, was because I didn't feel like hearing all of that. I didn't want you throwing the last wreck into my face. That's why I didn't tell you!" She said before fluffing her pillow and dropping her head.

"So, you thought it made sense to lie to me and say that the car only got towed? Don't you think I would of rather hear the truth from you than to hear about the truth from Facebook and the blogs?!" I asked her, not worrying about the bass in my voice.

Mercedez smacked her lips before turning over onto her stomach, placing the pillow over her head. She knew I hated being ignored but I wasn't about to force her to talk to me any longer. It would just end up with us fighting and I wasn't trying to go to work mad. *Shit.* I thought to myself as I checked the time on my watch; it was ten minutes till eight. I picked up my phone, placing it in my pocket, then lifted the pillow to try to look at her again. Mercedez was still on her stomach, with her eyes closed, pretending as though she was sleep. Maybe she thought that pretending to be sleep would make me leave her alone but if anything, it only irked me.

I swung my leather, cross body briefcase, across my chest before talking to her, one last time. "I'm going to work, but you need to get your shit together." She only groaned.

"I'm serious, Mercedez. Call me when you get up," I told her as I kissed her on the neck and placed the cover back over her body, closing the door and taking the banister of spiral stairs all the way up to the rooftop.

I lived in the family mansion with Mercedez along with my father, Cyrus. The mansion came with ten bedrooms, nine and a half bathrooms, a grand ballroom, a home library, an underground wine cellar, in house pool, outdoor pool, home theater, and a four-car garage. We lived in an elite community in the River Oaks area; the uptown part of Houston. I could only remember Cyrus getting married once and for a short period of time.

I met my stepmother, Joyce, and my stepbrother, Serpent, shortly before Mercedez came to live with me and Cyrus. Cyrus claimed his marriage didn't work because she wanted him to choose her over the business and that wasn't, something he was willing to do. After Cyrus had a separation, he dedicated himself full time to the oil business and rarely stepped foot in the mansion. He practically lived over at the office building. He'd never even been back there since his wife left. Mercedez and I were left to play house together. Imagine having a mansion to yourself as a teenager; That was just how it had always been.

I loved and cared about Mercedez; I would never want to do anything to break her heart. That was why I stayed down with her, because I didn't want to hurt her like the people in her past. I knew what she had been through. Parentless and living in the slums with the only blood relative that vouched to be her caretaker, her big cousin Bugatti; who was raising her and very protective over his little cousin. I'm talking about a nigga couldn't even look her way or he was asking for a fight.

Bugatti used to work for Cyrus before the oil business was booming. He ended up getting arrested while doing a run. That's when Cyrus came home and told me that Mercedez was moving in with us and that we were her family now. When I went to visit Bugatti in prison with Cyrus, he had asked me to watch over Mercedez while he was away and I thought I could, but that could only go so far. It didn't take a dummy to realize that Mercedez was developing into a young woman; pretty, popular, and rebellious. No longer being under Bugatti's watchful eye, she started partying, drinking and staying out late. It was like she didn't have any more rules.

When she came back to school the following year, everybody thought Mercedez and I were an item because they always saw me walking her to class or waiting for her after school. When really, I saw it as my duty to protect her because I'd given Bugatti my word. Like my father said, your word is everything.

Everybody was assuming we had sex when we didn't. At the time I thought she was too young, and I wanted to respect her as Bugatti's baby cousin. One night when she first stayed with us and came out of the bathroom, I was chilling on my bed when I saw her drop her towel in the hallway and I had kept my door close ever since. Then after prom, while everybody was spending the night at some hotel or going out to eat, I went straight home because I didn't have a prom date. I was sleeping in my bed when I heard the door to my bedroom creak open. Mercedez and I were the only two in the house, so I knew it was nobody else but her. I was half sleep when she slid under my covers and that's when I turned over to see that she was naked. I could have had sex with her, people probably thought I was crazy for not trying to hit, but I turned her down at the time. That didn't mean I couldn't hold her, but I was confused when she began crying. Still, I held her because I felt that was what she truly needed.

The next morning, when she wasn't in the bed, I got up to check on her and realized she was gone. When I called Cyrus and told him, he made it clear to me not to report her missing because she would go to Juvenile for being declared a runaway. So, I didn't go back to visit Bugatti because I didn't want to have to be the one to tell him that his cousin had run away.

Life had moved on, years had passed, and I thought I would never see Mercedez again. Until she showed up at the mansion one night telling me the reason she'd left Houston, was because she wanted to get a fresh start in a different city, which was why she had run away and was living in LA. When she said the only, reason she'd come back was because she truly loved me, I knew then what it was like to lose someone you loved because I'd witnessed my father go through it.

I took the stairs to the roof of the mansion and climbed into my chopper; my baby was a Bell Jet Ranger. Nearly costing me about one million, it was the most expensive item I'd ever purchased for myself. I directed the steering bar, taking flight to the largest oil facility known to men; *The Blackwells' Energy & Co.* It was the best feeling in the world to take an elevator to the top floor, where I had the best visual of the lone star state. Cyrus owned 90 percent of the oil well and energy business. We topped the charts as the number one competitor. Our main facility in Texas sat on 48 acres of land. The facility was equipped with thirty floors of built in offices, a fitness center, a day care center, cafeteria, a five-level parking garage, a library and of course the central plant, outside in the back of the building.

Working as a financial advisor, I liked to think of oil as a commodity. I did most of the financial planning and negotiations. Clients came to me when they wanted to negotiate deals on standard oil and gas. I was on my computer, in my office, comparing prices when my receptionist, Ms. Fiona's voice rung through the intercom.

"Good morning, Mr. True. Mr. Cyrus would like to see you in his office, pronto."

"Thank you, Fiona." I told her on the intercom, before walking out of my office and onto the elevator.

Nobody had ever heard Cyrus speak but the people that personally knew him, which wasn't many people. He was the type of businessmen to let his work speak for itself. Cyrus had rarely asked for me, so I knew it had to be something important. When I made it to his floor I walked to his office, knocking before closing the door behind me.

"You wanted to see me, father."

Cyrus was sitting at his cherry oak wood desk. The back of his leather executive chair was facing me, so I couldn't see his face.

"How are the Blackwell's supposed to set an example as the top rank in the oil business when you're late to work?"

"Cyrus I was only late by one min,"

"A minute that could of loss us an investment!" He spat, spinning around in his chair and bringing his fist down on the desk.

I wasn't surprised at my father's reaction. Cyrus was passionate when it came to the business, and even though he was counting on me to take his spot, I honestly didn't even want it. I had millions saved to one day invest in my own business; something in my name. Since my father had donated to charities, I wanted to come up with a business that would benefit people also, rather they were rich or poor. I just didn't know what. Cyrus got up, walking over to the floor to ceiling window with his hands balled behind his back. He didn't even look at me, but I could see that his face was hard as stone.

"I worked my fingers to the bone. You would never understand the sacrifice I went through to get this business off the ground. Don't ever in your life think just because you're my son and a Blackwell, that you get a pass to get off easily. You think people are gonna give you what you want of you ask em? HELL NO! THAT'S WHY YOU HAVE TO TAKE IT!!! This is a dog-eat-dog world and we have to work, day in and day out, in order to stay at the top of the food chain."

I didn't say anything. Throughout the years, I'd learned that it was just best to listen.

"You see all these people?" He asked me as I walked over to the floor to ceiling window, and gander my eyes down at the people walking in and out of the building.

"I see them." I acknowledged.

"Picture these people as tiny ants, and our business is the colony. The ant workers wouldn't know how to run a colony if it wasn't for the queen ant. That's where we come in. Without the queen ant, the ant workers, have no direction. Their sole purpose in life is to serve us." He said proudly.

The conversation was interrupted by the sound of Cyrus' extension phone ringing. He traveled over towards his desk, sitting back down. He answered the phone before placing the person on hold and cupping his hand over the lower end of the phone, motioning me out of the door.

"That's all for today, True." Cyrus told me as he turned back around in his executive chair.

I closed the door to his private office, stepping back onto the elevator and walking back into my office. That was the norm of my father and I's relationship. The difference between us is, I didn't see people that worked for the company as ants, I only saw people as people. Then again, that's just me.

Everybody wanted to be successful but didn't want to go through the struggle of doing the work. Unlike my son, True, life wasn't handed to me on a silver spoon and platter and as long as the Blackwell name was running through his veins, I had no issue reminding True of his wealthy privilege.

Just like a true hustler, I got it straight up out the mud! I was born into the life of crime as an adolescent; petty theft had caused me to have a few run ins with the law and I didn't stop getting into trouble till a couple of Og's schooled me by putting me under their wing. I had managed to crawl my way out of poverty, dropping out of high school to focus on dealing drugs full time. That's when I learned how to hustle my way into getting the best deals possible and how to get the most out of every nickel and dime. After a few trials and errors, I'd graduated from being a bottom feeder and standing on the corner selling baggies of weed, advancing my way up to becoming one of the youngest drug lords in history.

By the time I turned sixteen, I was running the biggest drug empire in Houston, making millions by distributing large shipments of the purest cocaine across the states. At the age of twenty-five, I had an abundance of cash that led me into purchasing some stocks and trade. I used the money from that to start a small drilling company. That was when I discovered that the biggest profit didn't come from drilling oil, it came from refining it. *The Blackwells' Energy & Co* was then created and built on a billion-dollar foundation. With that much power from handling oil, I had all different types of women who were willing to bow down and kiss the bottom of my feet. Women of all ages obeyed my every command and every night I was waking up in a bed full of women.

Eventually, responsibility was knocking at my door. True, the young king was then born. He didn't have any ties too his mother because he was the son of a high-priced prostitute. Most of the women I fooled around with back in the day were street walkers. Since street walkers didn't get attached, I got along with those types of women well. We both shared something in common and that was being focused on the dollar bill. When True's mother told me that she was expecting my child, I made her get a DNA test to prove that the baby was mine. True was only six days old when his mother gave me full custody, in return for a piece of crack rock. Pussy was all starting to feel the same to me and at one point, I wanted only one woman to love.

"Now you were saying?" I asked Mrs. Fiona as she repeated herself through the speaker of the business phone, sounding like she was in a panic.

"Sorry to bother you, sir, but a woman claiming to be your wife, by the name of Joyce Blackwell is here."

"Joyce Blackwell?" I questioned, scratching the stubble of my salt and pepper chin hair.

I hadn't heard that name in a long time. Joyce was the only woman who'd ever had a chance with my heart. Being the owner of a multi-billion, dollar company with a son to take look after, Joyce was hired as my help. She had to have been cleaning the mansion for months, but I had never took the time to notice her; Not till the day I saw her in the middle of the ballroom, on her hands and knees, scrubbing the shine in the floor. Her thick hair was pulled back and braided into a bun, showing off the feminine features in her face. Her luminous skin and chink slit eyes, told me that she was a Native, mixed with African descent.

She was dressed in this white collard maid outfit with an apron tied around her waist. The worn, down tennis shoes on her feet told me that she was a hardworking woman and the fact that my money didn't impress her, I wanted to make her mine.

I had moved Joyce and her son, Serpent, into the mansion but our marriage failed before it even begun. Let's just say, that she couldn't teach an old dog new tricks. The last time I'd heard from my wife, was when she called me the night that she was supposed to return home from the summer trip with Serpent, but she never did. She called me demanding for a separation, never even giving me an explanation of why she wanted us to split; which is why I refused to divorce her. When I threw all of her and Serpent clothes out on the street and didn't hear from neither one of them for some years, I was astonished when Serpent came to my office as a full-grown man. He asked for a job in need, so I made a deal to hire him under one condition; stay away from his stepbrother, True and to approach me as his boss, never his family.

"Joyce Blackwell is requesting to specifically speak to you." Fiona informed. "I told her that you were out of the office and asked her if she would like for me to take a message, but she's refusing to corroborate and says that she needs to speak to you now. Should I call security and have her escorted out of the building, sir?"

"No. Just bring her up." I responded before hanging up the phone.

I removed the frame that I kept on my desk of Joyce and I, placing the picture frame inside of my drawer before Joyce limped inside of my office, twenty minutes later.

"Long time no see, Cyrus." Joyce spoke as she sat in the black leather chair in front of my desk; laying her cane across her lap.

"My beloved wife, Joyce. What can I do for you?" I smiled and asked, lost as to why she was there.

My wife, who'd left me, had always been beautiful. With skin the shade of cayenne and a smile with a gap in the middle, that gave you a window to her soul; I was sad to say, she didn't look like the same Joyce that I had once fell in love with many years ago. She once had long vibrant hair, that was now dull and gray. Deep, crow's feet had surrounded her eyes and the most physical change was the right side of her face, that was sagging as if she'd suffered a stroke.

"The reason I came down here is because I need something from you. My insurance no longer covers my prescription and I hate to bother Serpent with my problems." She said as she beat around the bush.

"If money is what you need then why not just ask?" I said while taking out a brick of Benjamin's from the flap in the inside of my blazer, sliding the money across the desk. "Had we just worked out our marriage, you wouldn't have to come down here begging me for money."

"I could see that coming down here was a mistake. Remember that I'm your wife." Joyce said as she got up from the chair, with the assistance of her cane.

She was always a stubborn woman, which was why I had made her my wife. Even when she needed money, she'd rather hang on to her pride instead.

"Now wait a minute, Joyce, where's your sense of humor, baby?" I questioned as I got up to grab the same hand that was about to turn the metal doorknob; giving her a kiss on the back of her hand.

"I see that you haven't changed one bit." She said as she sighed. "You still think that your money can rule your way into my heart."

"My money hasn't shown me anything differently." I responded, handing her the stack of bills as she shoved it in her purse.

I sat against the desk and withdrew one of the fat, Cuban cigars from the cigar box. Sticking the gar inside of my mouth I flicked the gold lighter, adding the small flame.

"I see you're still wearing your wedding ring." She said while squinting her eyes in my direction.

"And why should I take it off? After all of these years, you never even gave me a reason to file for a divorce but tell me something, Joyce, how come you never came back to the mansion after you took Serpent on a camping trip? Was leaving to South Texas just some excuses to ask me for a divorce? What did I do that caused you to never come back home and call me from a phone, asking for a divorce?"

"You really think while I was gone away with Serpent on a camping trip, I'd just come up with some excuse to leave you and ask for a divorce?" She spat. "Cyrus, I thought you was smarter than that. By this time, you should know what you did. You want to know why I decided to leave you for good? I'll give you a hint," She said as she gave me a faint grin. "It involves you and a younger woman. I want you to think on that," Joyce said before leaving out of my office.

My mind went back to the first night I invited a younger woman into the mansion. There was no way they could have known about me sleeping with a minor because her and Serpent had never come back from the camping trip; Or did she?

Mercedez Lauren Taylor

If only True knew when I wrecked my jeep by running into a ditch, I was really trying to kill myself. This smile behind my bright pretty face could have fooled anybody; hell, I almost fooled my damn self. To the outside world it looked as though I was enjoying the place in my life, but it was bittersweet because Bugatti wasn't free to enjoy it with me. Being the fiancé of an upcoming billionaire had gained me the status, fame and popularity I'd been dreaming of since I was a little girl. I thought the best decision Bugatti could have ever done for me was to send me to live with the Blackwell's; the most, wealthiest socialites in Texas. Everybody who was somebody, wished that they could walk a day in my shoes; if they only knew the dream came with a price.

When True was pressing me about the car it wasn't that I was trying to ignore him, I was just tired of looking him in the eye and lying to him.

Part of the story that I told True wasn't a lie. I was at The Marriott Hotel and had been drinking, but I didn't go there for a modeling gig and I wasn't there with my friends either.

When I didn't hear the propellers to True's loud ass chopper anymore, I knew he had made it to work by now. I pulled the covers back and snatched my phone out of the socket of the charger. Eager to look up all of the new gossip and rumors that were affiliated with my name, I went to Media Takeout and scrolled through the pictures from when I use to be a video vixen, down to the leaked video from the night of my arrest. I needed to see what all the trolls had to say about me. I love being the center of attention, especially on social media. Only because it made me feel relevant, compared to True who liked keeping a low profile. I hate splitting my time with him and the fuckin office, but his money kept me busy.

After I lounged around for an hour, watching the re-runs of my favorite reality television show Love and Hip-hop Holly-wood, I got myself together before walking down to my two-story dressing room to pick an outfit for the day. I went with a black long sleeve, plaid mini skirt, Gucci waist belt, knee length leather boots and a cross body Gucci purse. Being an upcoming celebrity, meant I had certain standards to keep up with and when I wasn't modeling and promoting the fashion shows, I was hanging out and shopping at the luxury boutiques with my friends.

Since my jeep was wrecked and my second DUI restricted me from driving, I buzzed for a private chauffeur to me pick me up in the front of the mansion. As I slid into the backseat, I took my cell phone from out of my purse and dialed my best friend, Diamond's number.

===

"Bout time you called me. I forgot to tell you that the leaked video of your arrest has made you hit a million fol-lower's on Instagram too!" Diamond acknowledged.

She was a moderator for all, of my social media platforms, so we would usually talk about it over the phone. Her and my other best friend, Princess, were the only two I trusted to con-fined in. Other than True, I didn't have a lot of real friends be-cause most of my friends were fake and only saw me as a stuck up, snotty bitch. Diamond and Princess were the only two real friends I had.

"Dime, meet me at the outlet in River Oaks." I told her be-fore hanging up the phone.

Twenty-five minutes later, I walked through the court-yard of the mall and saw Diamond with Princess in *Pretty Little*

Things boutique, searching through the racks of clothes. They both had occupations as sugar babies; getting spoiled by rich old men who were in love with young pussy were their expertise.

"What's been up with you, Mrs. Billion Dollar Blackwell?" Asked Diamond, as she hugged me before taking a few pieces of clothing with her into the dressing room.

Princess came over and gave me a side hug with more clothes for Diamond to try on, ready to rate her outfits as she threw the clothes over her dressing room door.

"Yeah, you know the only time you hit us up to go therapy shopping, is when something is bothering you." Princess chimed in and said.

Diamond and Princess were the only two people who knew about me battling with depression. They knew it was mainly about Bugatti because he was the only living family member I had, and he was also somebody that I knew I could trust. True and my friends thought I didn't go to see Bugatti because I couldn't stand to see him in jail. Truth is, when he got locked up on a twenty-year sentence in federal prison, sending me to live with the Blackwell's, I thought that everything in my life would be good. I thought I was finally going to get the life I deserved. The first night I came to live with the Blackwell's, Cyrus walked me into the huge foyer of the mansion and handed me this picture frame. He pointed to his wife, saying they were on a camping trip and wasn't expected to come home until later that night. Letting me know that when they did, I'd get a chance to meet them.

I had already known of his stepson from school; only because a lot of people use to call him Snake for short. When Cyrus then called True downstairs, he made him show me to my room upstairs, right down the hall from his. When I first start living with True, I had developed a crush on him. He'd known Bugatti before he knew me and maybe he thought I was just too young. I remember walking out of the bathroom, right after I'd taken a shower; True was in his room. I dropped my towel on purpose just to see what his reaction was going to be. I thought he would smile or flirt with me but when he didn't. It was the first time I didn't get a reaction out of a guy. I knew True had seen me but he just got up and politely closed his door.

That night I went to bed I thought it was True that I heard opening the door and walking into my room but when the person got under the covers, opening my legs and eating my pussy out, I knew that it wasn't True. It was Cyrus who was kissing all over me like I was his wife. I was scared, only because I'd never had an older man touch my body like that, and I couldn't say that I wasn't enjoying it, because I was. It made me feel like a woman. At the time I thought that was the attention that I wanted from a man. Cyrus and I ended up having sex in my bed but whenever I tried to kiss him back, he wouldn't let me; he couldn't even look at me. His penis had hurt a little but not much, only because I was already having sex with boys at school whenever I could.

When he was grinding on top of me he stopped during sex and admission, saying that he wouldn't be able to look at me without telling me the real reason he took me. Cyrus said when Bugatti went to jail doing a job for him, the laws had confiscated millions in Bugatti's car that belonged to him. Cyrus told Bugatti that he only had two choices to pay off his debt; Either get killed behind bars or sell his most prized possession. That prized possession was me. He said if I ever tried to bribe him over this and make a claim to the police, he would have no choice but to kill me. That he would be able to get away with it because nobody would come searching for me. Who knew that my life had any value? I was nothing to Cyrus but his property and Bugatti only saw me as a pawn. When Cyrus had finished having sex with me, I could have sworn I saw a shadow move under the door but maybe it was just my imagination. I expected to meet his wife and stepson by the end of the night, but I never did. I didn't know why but I could take a guess. Maybe because his wife knew his ass was a cheater.

After that night, Cyrus told me that from that night forward, I had to have sex with him in his office; Like it was my job. That's the real reason Cyrus no longer came around the mansion; he was trying to hide his true intentions. Sex, partying and drugs became my coping mechanisms. Somehow alcohol had filled a void in my life that people around me couldn't. When I turned seventeen, I made it up in my mind that I was going to run away. Go somewhere, far, far away, where nobody knew me. That night before I left, I crept into True's bedroom. I knew he had just come back from prom, because his nicely stitched tux was on the gold floor. I'd just taken a shower, so my hair was still wet and dripping onto my naked body. I woke him up by kissing him, thinking my body could persuade him into have sex with me but True had turned me down; only allowing me to cry into his arms.

I spilled out all, of my emotions and True held me like he cared, rubbing my hair as he kissed me on my forehead. He held me until we both fell asleep. He was the only person who intentions were pure. When I woke up in his arms, I knew it was time for me to leave because I was depending on him emotionally. With a dream to stardom, I packed a suitcase and caught the Grey Hound with Princess and Diamond to Los Angeles. I wanted to tell True goodbye, but it would have been too hard. I always felt guilty for leaving True alone in that mansion by himself. With Cyrus in the office, he basically had to raise himself.

Well, one thing I soon realized was that a pretty face could only get you so far. Living in California it was a million girls who looked like me, and we were all competing for one spot. Being a former video vixen, I tried to sleep my way to the top. I decided to move in with a man I met on the set of one of his music videos. His name was Snow, he was a rapper originally from Inglewood. After we had been fucking for only two weeks, he said that he loved me and moved me into his penthouse in Hollywood. I thought I'd hit the jackpot, but Snow wasn't good for me. He got me hooked on all type of shit, including cocaine; I had taken a deal with the devil. A battle I was losing because I was too far gone.

Snow eventually became an abusive narcissist and being addicted to drugs, he had run out of money; which meant that I also, had no money. I was a coke addict who had hit rock bottom. Tired of living on the tough streets of LA, Diamond and Princess had moved back to Houston and told me that I could stay with them. Being an addict, I knew I couldn't get off the drugs cold turkey, so I called my legal guardian, Cyrus, who ended up reminding me that I would always belong to him, no matter how far I ran.

Cyrus ended up sending me to rehab where I got clean. When I went back to the mansion and saw True, I knew I wanted to be with him. I knew he was still single, known around Texas as one of the richest bachelors in the state, and I wanted his heart. When I brought the idea up of us being engaged, I went as far as swiping True's black card, purchasing a diamond ring from a customized jeweler. The media had declared us engaged and True had never denied it. We were expected to get married after he took over his father's business, but I was also expecting something else.

"Hello? Earth to Mercedez," Diamond asked as she came out of the dressing room snapping her fingers, bringing me out of my thoughts. When I glared at her, she was giving me this crazy look before posing in the mirror, while adjusting the clothing.

"Did you and True get into it again? Did he break off the engagement?"

"No." I said. "I needed ya'll to meet me because I thought you two would like to be the first to know that I'm pregnant." I announced; only nobody was cheering.

"Bitch is you serious right now?!" Princess yelled, almost dropping the mountain of clothes as she came over to me. "Whatever happened to you not wanting kids? And I thought you told me that you was on birth control?"

"And I was." I stated while giving her the eye roll. "But the Mirena had expired and it was starting to make me gain weight. It had already been in me for like five years, so I had made a decision to have it taken out like a year ago."

I'd never brought up taking my birth control out to True because I wanted to have a baby by him. He practiced safe sex religiously and because of that, he made it hard. I didn't even know why I was sitting up there trying to explain myself to my friends because at the end of the day, I was a grown woman.

"And you know for sure that you're pregnant?" Princess inquired.

"What am I? Dumb?" I sarcastically asked. "Of course, I know I'm pregnant! I wouldn't have called you two down here if I wasn't. When I had the Mirena in, I had my period every two to three months and when I took the birth control out, my period never came; I thought it was normal for me. I ended up going in for a check-up and a pregnancy test confirmed it. I'm pregnant, alright. Pregnant with a capitol P." I guess Princess sensed my attitude because she was now trying to ask me questions in a gentle tone.

"But you told True the news, right?" There was a long pause. I didn't like lying to my real friends, so I told the truth.

"Not exactly. You see I haven't told True because I'm not pregnant by him, I'm pregnant by somebody else." I confessed as Diamond and Princess traded glances at each other.

"Oh, shit girl, well who cares?" Diamond shrugged. "No one has to know but us."

"But that's just it, I don't want to keep something like this away from True. And my real baby daddy deserves to know; I don't want to keep the secret away from him either." I added.

"Well do the nigga at least have money?" They both asked in unison, waiting for my response.

"Since when will money ever become a problem for me?" I stood there and asked.

"You're not actually going to risk telling True that the baby isn't his? He'll kick you out of the mansion and will be sporting another bitch on his arm."

"I doubt it." I said with squinted eyes and a twisted lip.

True wasn't even like that. I knew him well enough to know that he would never do anything intentionally to hurt me, and he didn't fuck around on me like that. He was too committed to me and his job.

"Then why would you give all of that up to have a baby with somebody else?" Diamond asked.

I knew it probably doesn't make logical sense, but we're talking about a whole child here. I thought.

"After you marry True and become Mrs. Blackwell, you'll be sitting court side with the other celebrity couples. Maybe even getting a chance to sit with Jay-Z and Bey." Princess pointed out.

"You want my advice, sis?" Diamond said. "What True doesn't know won't hurt him."

"Easier said than done." I replied as we continued shopping.

I wanted to believe what my friends were telling me, but I'd left a small detail out. I was pregnant by somebody True knew. I was pregnant by his stepbrother, Serpent and the bad part about all of it was, even though I knew that he didn't give two shits about me, the fact that he was willing to keep a hold on all of my secrets, had somehow made me fall in love with him. At the same time, I didn't want to lose the first guy who had taken care of my heart, which was True.

Done shopping with the girls, I got into the service vehicle and was just about to head back to the mansion, when I got an urgent text from Cyrus, stating that he wanted to see me.

"I need to take a detour to the Blackwell's Energy & Co facility." I told the driver, who then nodded and turned the vehicle around, making it towards the freeway. I had gotten use to fucking Cyrus because just like any other job, in order to get paid, I had to follow his specific guidelines.

I took off the boots I had on my feet, going into the bag of gear that I had just bought from the boutique. I slipped each foot into some white, knee length stockings, taking out a pair of leather heels and placing a heel on each foot. With my back against the seat I raised my butt up, giving me enough room to slip my panties down my knees. I teased my hair into two pig tails, before catching the driver's baffled stare.

"What the fuck are you looking at you perv!" I spat at the nosey driver, before glimpsing out of the window to see that I was at the facility.

I added a pair of glasses to my face, swinging my thirteen-inch heels out of the vehicle. I was dressed like a little schoolgirl as I walked towards the side of the building where it was a blind spot to others, catching the employee service elevator to the top floor of the building. I got off of the elevator and down the hallway to Cyrus's office. Since his door was cracked open and he wasn't in sight, I walked inside of the office, going around to the back of the room, where it was this door to a sex dungeon. I went inside of the sex room overloaded with all type of sex toys, whips and torture weapons that was hanging on the walls. In the corner of the room was a bed that I knew so well, because Cyrus and I had sex in that same bed. I kneeled onto the floor in front of the bed like the slave I was, patiently waiting for Cyrus to enter the room.

The door creaked open and I could hear the sole of Cyrus's shoes shuffle as he came inside of the room, walking slowly across the floor. I could smell his expensive cologne. For Cyrus to be an old man in his seventies, he had the possessive sexual stamina of twenty-seven, year old. He didn't look like he had aged at all. He kept a trimmed fade with a salt and pepper beard on his lower chin. I could see the outline of his broad shoulders in his custom formal suit, with charcoal colored eyes that was liable to put you under a trance.

He took a black spike collar from off of one of the hooks tacked on the wall, walking over to me and kneeling down to latch the collar around my neck; before pecking me on my lips as he played in my pig tails.

"On your feet slave." He ordered as he sat down on the bed.

I got up and walked over to him as he played with his pants, unbuckling the Versace belt, as the weight of his pants clunked down to his ankles.

"Suck this dick, you slave." Cyrus rudely commanded.

My two hands jacked off his dick until I felt the hardness in his penis. I opened my slobbering mouth, wrapping my tight lips around the head of his tip, just like I would on a blow pop. As I sucked his dick, I could see feel his hands motion behind his head. He grunted as his back fell across the mattress of the bed.

"Suck that dick harder you dirty little girl." He groaned while I twisted my hands faster around his dick.

"Are you ready to taste the white frosting?" Cyrus asked as his hands yanked at the both of my pig tails. I nodded with his dick in my mouth, ready to catch his heavy load.

"Get ready, here it comes. Arggggh!" He whined in ecstasy, as I tasted a flow of his dead sperm seeping into the crevice of my mouth.

I swallowed and wiped the smear of his cum from my mouth, not saying a word as he sat up to unlatch the collar from around my neck. In exchange for my sexual pleasure, every meeting, Cyrus wired money over to my account and I transfered that money into Bugatti's account in prison. Even though I was having a hard time trying to forgive Bugatti for what he had done to me, sending that money to his account had somehow confirmed to me that he was alright.

"Should I come the same time next week?" I asked Cyrus as he got himself together.

"Same time next week." He repeated. "That's all I wanted for today." He said before I called for a vehicle to pick me up and drop me back off at the mansion.

<h1 style="text-align:center">Serpent</h1>

After I texted Zonnique to let her know how I couldn't wait for us to tie the knot, I headed out into the open parking lot of the oil and energy facility. Normally Zonnique would have fixed me a lunch for work but since we stayed out late after the proposal, she only had time to get Zion to school before the teacher marked him tardy. I loved Zonnique but sometimes she forgot that a nigga had needs too.

When I received a text to come through, I started my ride and drove towards the Texas millionaire's road; right off, of River Oaks, where you could see the mega mansion that took up the entire block. As I made it to the entrance of the French gates, I dialed in the code while waiting for assistance.

"Who is it?" The voice from the other end of the speaker said with an attitude.

I licked my lips and playfully mugged the speaker, like someone could see me. "Man stop playing, you know exactly who it is." I said back and grinned.

The voice chuckled. "I just wanted to hear you say your name. That's all," she sung. "Come in and just park in the back, Serpent." The voice responded before the speaker cut off, buzzing the French iron gates open to let me in.

I drove down the private road, passing the lake and around the circular driveway; parking all the way in the back in front of nicely trimmed trees, surrounding the fenced in barricade. When I got out of the car, I turned my phone off before knocking on the door three times. The door swung open, and a fine dime was waiting for me inside.

"You ready to eat, daddy? Oh, I hope you didn't really think I meant food." Mercedez was leaning on the door with her long, tan, legs, and an expensive Japanese floral robe loosely tied around her thin waist, smelling like she had just gotten out of the shower.

The red lipstick coated on her lips and the two buns pinned up on each side of her head, with a pair of chop sticks sticking out on each side, made her look like one of them Geisha's straight out of China. She looked foreign from her pale colored breast, dime sized nipples, all the way down to her slim waist and bald pussy.

If I wasn't in love with Zonnique, Mercedez would have had me pussy whipped. If we were in a different time zone, maybe she would have had a chance to really be with a nigga.

"I know you ain't wear all of that for me, girl?" I said, smacking her ass as she gazed back at me, while striking a model pose.

"Well, who else would I wear it for? You and I are the only two here."

Mercedez wasn't no brains and beauty like Zonnique, but she was the definition of a bad bitch. I'm talking about everybody and they daddy wanted to hit that. I had seen her face in a couple music videos and magazines here and there, even heard through the grapevine that she had got strung out on dope but seeing her in person, I would've never guessed that she previously used crack.

The other night when we ended up fucking inside of that hotel and Mercedez had too much to drink, I was still thinking about what she had told me; How her cousin sold her to Cyrus when she was just a teen and how I could use that to my advantage. She made me promise not to tell anyone, right before fighting me for her keys and storming out of the hotel. That's when I knew, Mercedez and I had something in common; we both wanted Cyrus Blackwell dead.

Mercedez's body was light as a feather, as I walked up the banister of curved stairs, throwing her onto the middle of the bed. I unhooked her robe, as her small breast bounced freely. She laid on her back, trying to hide her pussy by covering it up with her hands.

"Serpent, wait." Mercedez whined.

"Wait for what?" I asked. I didn't know why she was acting as if she was shy, knowing I'd fucked her in every hole. "Just let me smell that pussy right quick. I growled. "Let me see if that motherfucker tastes as good as it smells." I took a sniff at her cave, before snaking my tongue around her pink clit.

Yeah it was wrong that I was cheating on Zonnique with my stepbrother's fiancé, but I got a thrill out of fucking something that belonged to True. Mercedez was looking for the attention to be fucked and I was willing to give it to her.

"Serpent I said wait," Mercedez demanded, her fingers clawing at my scalp.

"What you mean wait? Man stop playing with me and open this pussy up, girl." I told her as she tried to run. If it wasn't for me locking her legs in place, she would've squirmed right off of the bed.

"Shit." She groaned loudly, as her body begin to tremble; hinting that she was about to cum in my mouth. I sped up the momentum with my tongue. I knew I was hitting Mercedez's spot the way her grip got tighter around my head.

"Serpent I'm, I'm, I'M PREGNANT!" She blurted before her body went still.

"You what? Why the fuck you ain't tell me bout this shit

when we met up the other night?" I hissed, suddenly turned off because my dick was now limp. Mercedez sat up on the bed like she didn't mean to tell me the way she had, looking all lost and shit.

"I didn't know how to tell you at the time," She muttered.

"Yeah okay." I said but to me, that wasn't no fuckin excuse.

"Fuck Mercedez! You got me all up in this nigga's bed, eating out your pussy, just to tell me that you pregnant?"

She said nothing, only looking at me with them jolly green eyes. I got up wiping the cum off my lips, fixing my clothes, as I walked down the banister of stairs. I had already been there long enough.

"So, what Serpent? You just gone bounce like we haven't been fucking for over a year now?" Mercedez spat, following behind me with her A sized tits, bouncing up and down.

Even though she looked real fuckable, I was too mad to focus on that. Now that she had gave me that dreading news, I needed to figure out how I was going to get out of the situation.

With my hand on the front doorknob, my back turned from her as I said, "I hope you don't, think it's mine because if it is, you might as well claim yourself as a single mother. Don't wait to have the baby to think that I would claim it, because I won't. Straight up. Either tell True it's his or I'll pay for the abortion, but that's it." I told her.

Mercedez got in my face like she was looking for a fight. "Oh, I get it." She said nodding like she was answering herself. "You wanna grow up and be like Cyrus. Your feelings must really be hurt that he didn't claim you as his step on."

My jaw clenched because she knew how I felt about that, Zonnique didn't even know that I had a stepbrother. Mercedez was pushing it and I knew exactly what I needed to say to keep her feelings in check.

"Girl, you fuckin crazy if you think I'm bout to risk tellin my girl that I got my stepbrother's fiancé pregnant. How you think that shit sound? I just proposed to her and you sitting here talking bout you pregnant with my baby? You want the both of us to end up on fatal attraction? When you find out how many weeks you is, I'll pay for however much the abortion cost; I don't give a fuck what you do after that. Rather you keep the baby or abort it, that's not my problem, it's yours. With that being said," I closed the door behind me and bounced.

I was re-reading the text message that Serpent had sent me, blushing all over again because he was just as excited as I was to finally be getting married. I had made it to class only fifteen minutes late, trying not to yawn because I'd crammed in an early morning of studying. I was casual in a cinnamon-spiced crew neck, bleached jeans, and off-white Chuck Taylor's to match. I was skimming through my notes while Professor Daniel's lectured about the physics of ultrasound for the past hour and a half. I couldn't stop glancing down at my engagement ring, still in shock that I would soon be Mrs. McKinney.

Serpent and I had agreed that we wouldn't start planning the wedding until after I graduated, which meant we would be getting married just in time for the holidays. I wanted to get married on Christmas to show Zion that we would be a complete family.

When class let out, I was the last one to get out of my seat. My phone dinged from the group chat I shared with my friends, Brooke and Myrah. They were both responding to the picture I'd sent of me holding up my hand while pointing to my ring, with this jarring expression on my face.

Brooke: *Congrats Nique! I hope you know I plan to be a bridesmaid! This isn't up for debate...*

Myrah: *Congratulations Zonnique! We need to start planning...LIKE RIGHT NOW!*

I giggled, replying with plans to go shopping for my wedding dress the next time we all had a chance to meet. I tapped out of the group chat and walked towards the door, passing up Professor Daniel's, who'd looked up from the stack of papers he was grading at his desk.

"Miss Zonnique Jones, if you want to qualify for my internship program, working aside me as my ultrasound tech at my family practice, you must first ace the midterms in order to become a finalist. And by doing that, you have to come on time. You have to pay attention and you have to stay up in this class." He said, giving me a stern look.

"I know Professor Daniel's," I said, tucking my phone into my back pocket and swinging my backpack over one shoulder. "I can make it on time. I had just overslept and was rushing out of the door this morning to at least get my son to,"

"Zonnique, I know you come from a good family. You know I went to med school with your father before we both opened our own practices. I'm expecting you to pass your midterms and be on the list. Don't let me down." He noted with a straight face.

I thought about Professor Daniel's comment as I drove to Zion's school. I got into one of the carpool lines, where teachers were gathering up their students and walking them to their parent's vehicles. All of the wedding talk had me thinking about how I missed my parents more than ever. Other than marrying Serpent, all I really wanted was for my parents to be at my wedding. It wouldn't be right if my father wasn't there to walk me down the aisle. It wouldn't feel right if my mother couldn't give me something old, something new, something borrowed and something blue.

I had gotten over them kicking me out because I understood that I was grown. Being a mother to a child, I wanted Zion to meet all, of his grandparents; not just Mama Joyce. Plenty of times I thought about just showing up to their house with Zion, but what if they wouldn't accept him? It was one thing to turn me away but I couldn't put Zion through that. He was just an innocent child.

The car behind me honked, startling me as I eased on the gas while moving up in the line of cars. I could see Zion skipping with his flailing shoelaces as he waved at me. I waved at him back. The teacher walked him down to my car before opening the car door.

"MOMMY!" Zion shouted.

He was smiling with a gap from his two top missing teeth and sliver caps, climbing into his booster seat, as he stuffed his mouth with a handful of gummy bears that I kept in his cup holder. I waved goodbye to his teacher before driving onto the street.

"Hey Zion, put your seat belt on." I urged because the school police were quick to pull somebody over for a ticket.

"Where are we going, mama?" Zion asked as his feet kicked the back of my seat.

"We're going to go see daddy." I said as I got on the forty-five freeway, driving to Serpent's job.

I wanted to surprise Serpent with a lunch date because the three of us hadn't spent time together in a while. Zion and I had been up to his job a couple of times because I would sometimes bring Serpent food. Every time I went up here with Zion, he'd always enjoy playing inside of the library that was in the facility. After I parked on the second floor of the parking garage, I took Zion's hand and we got onto the elevator that led us inside of the building.

Wanting to meet Serpent for his lunch, I headed to the cafeteria. Walking towards the food service counter with a tray, I placed down a half sub sandwich, a fruit salad, and two bottles of water. I added a meatball marina sub for Serpent. Zion only wanted two cheeseburger sliders and an apple juice box.

As I paid the cashier for our food, I sat down at a round table. While Zion chomped down on his burger, I knew Serpent only had an hour to eat so I tried calling him a few times, lost at why his phone kept going straight to voicemail. I thought maybe his phone had died but then again, Serpent couldn't have his phone on him while he was out there on the plant, so it wouldn't make sense for his phone to be dead.

I was done eating in thirty minutes and even though I wanted to leave, I still wanted to let Serpent know that we'd come. I got up from my chair walking to the security booth, asking for a McKinney. The security personnel shuffled through papers.

"Sorry ma'am, but Serpent McKinney is out on lunch; left about two hours ago."

Two Hours? Where the hell did Serpent need to go for two hours?

"Does that mean we won't be seeing daddy at his job today?" Zion asked, tugging on my arm. I tried to force a smile on his behalf,

"Sorry, Zee, not today. But if you're still up by the time daddy gets home, I'll let you stay up an hour pass your bedtime; maybe he can even read you a bedtime story."

A gloomy expression appeared on Zion's face. Probably because he knew that he would be sleep by the time Serpent would even make it home. As we walked towards the lobby, Zion's eyes gleamed as he heard laughter from the children playing around in the library.

"Can we go, mama?! Oh please...please...please; with a cherry on top?!" Zion pleaded, making the cutest expression with his big brown puppy eyes. Something I could never resist.

"Why not?" I said.

Zion was pumped as he ran over to the touch screen computers, placing a pair of children friendly earphones on. It was no point of making a blank trip and it was the perfect time for me to study. I took a seat at one of the tables in the children's section, taking out my study guide and a couple of high lighters out of my backpack. An hour had passed by and I'd went through my study guide and read three chapters of a romance book. Taking out my cell, I tried phoning Serpent again before shoving it in my back pocket. That was going to be my last time calling him because he was irritating me.

"Come on, Zion." I called out.

I checked out some books by some of my favorite author's, like Octavia Butler and Mary Monroe. I even checked out a few children books for Zion. I stuffed my library card into my pocket-sized wallet, with a hand full of books in my arms.

"Race you to the car, Mama! Tag you're it!" Zion tapped me and zipped out of the library so fast, that I didn't even have time to place my books into my backpack.

"Zion, wait!"

When I went running after him like a bat out of hell, I tripped over my own two feet, falling flat on my face and sending all my books into the air. Zion was already outside in the libraries parking lot, but he had enough sense to know to come back if he didn't see me. If that fall wasn't embarrassing enough, I was now getting awkward stares from every direction of eyes in the building. Standing up to recover myself, I dusted myself off before bracing on my knees to scatter for all, of my items.

"Looks like you took a hard fall. My name's True; I just met your son Zion."

I tucked my hair behind my ear to clear my peripheral vision, turning my attention to a tall, handsome man. He was clean cut with a midrange stubble, golden bronze skin, and his eyes were dark as coals. He'd caught me off guard as he got on one knee beside me, dressed down in a formal suit. There was plenty of other men who'd passed me up in the building, yet he was the only one who offered to help. I thought that said a lot about a man.

"Sorry, Mama." Zion apologized, as he appeared behind True with a sympathetic frown. "But Mama, I saw the coolest thing when I was outside! Would you believe it was a helicopter on top of the building? IT WAS LIKE THIS BIG!" Zion yelled with his hands and arms out. "Mr. True said if I can ask you, my mom, to come with us to see the helicopter, he could take me on the top of the rooftop to see it. So, can we go see it mama? Oh, please mama, please?!"

True intervened. "Here. Let me help you with that. Sometimes I forget how big this place is when I'm in the office." He said while gathering up my books.

My lips slightly curled upwards. "I'd forgotten how big this place was myself." I told him. "We were only supposed to come into the facility to eat, but Zion wanted to play, and I decided to study; somehow I just got lost in a world of books inside of the library. I don't know how I even ended up checking out nine books." I giggled. He scrutinized his eyes at me curiously. His demeanor seemed inviting and True.

"I'm sorry, I don't think I ever caught you name." He said.

"Zonnique Jones." I told him.

"Zonnique what are you studying?"

"I'm studying to become a prenatal ultrasound technician."

His brows roused upwards; maybe he was impressed.

"You must really enjoy reading?" He pointed out, holding up one of my books to look at the front of the cover. "I try to read as often as I could, but working full-time, being cooped up in the office, I don't never find the time to."

"That's why you have to make time." I responded as I finished placing all, of my items into my backpack.

When he handed me back the book, we brushed hands, but I tried to play it off, still embarrassed from the fall I'd just taken in public.

"How about you take a book for yourself?" I told him, handing him a book called The Upper Room, by Mary Monroe. I had already read the book twice.

He smiled, placing the book under one arm. True dimples were deeper than mine. As we both stood up, he was looking at me as I wondered what he was thinking about; but I didn't know him well enough to ask.

"So, Mama, can we go see the helicopter?" Zion asked, his pleading eyes told me that he wouldn't let it go.

"No Zion. I'm sure Mr. True has to get back to work. And besides it's time for us to get back home. Don't you think we've had enough of an adventure for one day?"

"I don't mind showing you two the helicopter. I still have about an hour for lunch." He said, glancing down for the time on his Rolex. "I promised Zion that he could see it if you said yes. We just have, to take the employee stairs up to the roof. If that's fine with you." True offered.

"Fine with me. As long as you lead the way."

I'd just met Zion and learned Zonnique's name, yet I wanted to know more about Zion's mother. what was I thinking? I had a fiancé waiting on me at home. Zonnique's sweet smile was contagious. Her thick grade of hair flowed majestically down her back; her hazelnut coffee complexion, Hennessey colored eyes, upper dark lip, short and curvy body type, had me at hello. It turned me on that her favorite hobby involved reading. Zonnique was brains and beauty. No doubt, she was probably the whole package if you asked me.

"THIS IS SO COOL!" Zion jumped in excitement as we made it on top of the rooftop. He was so well mannered that he didn't even touch the chopper; only stared at it like a kid in the candy store. I walked him up to it, taking out the keys to unlock the door.

"If you think the outside is cool, wait until you see this," I opened the door to my helicopter and watched as his eyes widened.

"WOW!" Zion said in amazement, feeling all on the leather material of my three-seater.

Zonnique was watching us, as Zion sat in the front seat. He was so into it he began pressing buttons and making airplane noises. He even took a hold of the handheld radio, talking in it like he was communicating with another pilot. I allowed him to pretend as I glanced back at Zonnique, she slid her hands in the back pockets of her jeans as she took in a breath of air; like she could finally relax and breathe. Either Zonnique was memorized by the view of mixed color of blue clouds in the evening sky, or she had something else on her mind. The view up there could just about steal your breath away. You could see the skyline of Houston, which was why I'd always went up there whenever I needed to take a break.

Still wanting to get to know her, I turned to her and asked, "What made you want to become a prenatal ultrasound technician?"

She moved towards me, but she didn't take her eyes off, of Zion. As the chill swayed her hair in the wind, I thought she favored Bernice Burgos as she began to talk.

"While I was pregnant with Zion, I realized how much I cared about people and how important it was to be there for someone who's expecting."

Zonnique's smile then faded. Something was bothering her, and I was sure that if she was comfortable enough, then maybe she would tell me. I wasn't going to force it out of her though. She must've been cold because her lips were quivering. I took off my blazer and swung it over her shoulders. We were close enough to embrace but because she didn't know me, I didn't want to overstep my place. I just wanted her to know that I was there, and I was willing to listen if she needed me to.

She deeply sighed and said, "My parents and I haven't exchanged words to one another in about five years. After I told them I was pregnant with Zion, we haven't talked since he was born. Now my son is five and I'm about to be married." She said with her eyes on her ring, as she began fiddling with the diamond ring around her finger.

"I really want my parents to be in my wedding, hell I want them in Zion's life, but I don't know if they would even accept me or him."

Damn. And I thought I had problems with my father.

"Five years is a long time to go without seeing your family. I'm sure they miss you and wouldn't want to miss the chance to see their grandson grow up, let alone see their daughter get married. I know you must miss em terribly," When I said that, Zonnique turned around with her hands covering her face; I stepped in front of her.

"Are you okay?" I asked.

Her face was now buried into my chest. The way her shoulders shrugged had told me that she was crying. Maybe she didn't want Zion to see her crying? I embraced her with a bear hug like she was my lover, working my hands up to her face. Her watery eyes blinking up at me.

Damn this woman! Never mind that she'd just told me that she was engaged to be married. We were both engaged, and both belonged to somebody else. Zonnique sniffed, focusing back on Zion; she laughed as if the moment she'd just had, had caught her off guard.

"I don't usually do that when I first meet someone. Anyways, enough about me. I want to know about you." Zonnique said. "How do you like working for this company?"

I hate working for my father's company! Was what I wanted to tell her but every time somebody found out that I was the son and next in line to takeover, the multi-million, dollar company, the vibe would turn to something forced.

So Instead I said, "Truthfully, I've been in my office thinking about venturing off into my own company."

"I say you go for it then," Zonnique said. When we exchanged looks and looked back at Zion, he was asleep in the front seat.

"The excitement of the helicopter must've got to him." I said as I opened the door, adjusting the seat back so his mother could get to him.

Zonnique handed me back my blazer before picking Zion up and carrying him in her arms. When Zion's head slowly drooped onto her right shoulder, his finger's interlocked around his mother's neck. I threw my coat over the little guy for extra comfort, before walking with Zonnique to the second floor of the parking garage, to her car. As she stepped onto her tippy toes, fastening Zion into his booster seat, I was trying to be a gentleman, but I couldn't help but to look at her heart shaped ass.

"Bye-bye, Mr. True." Zion yawned and whispered, before falling back to sleep.

Meeting Zonnique and her son made me wonder what it would be like to have a child and a family of my own. Cyrus said that the business came first and that I had plenty of time to have kids when I retired. Mercedez and I had spoken about a baby in the past, but she always said that she wasn't the mothering type.

When I left the office, I went inside of the house that was dimmed, with a trail of candles that lead up the stairs and into the bedroom. When I opened the door, Mercedez was naked, spread out on the bed like she had been waiting on me forever.

"You did this for me, Cedez?" I asked as I sat my brief case on the floor and undid my suit and tie.

"I just wanted to give you a nice bubble bath; maybe makeup for this morning. I can't remember the last time you ever came home this early though." She said while unbuckling my belt and unzipping my pants.

As my penis sprung out of the hole of my boxers, Mercedez took ahold of my limber, gliding her hands up and down my shaft.

"I finished up early at the office." I explained as Mercedez got down on her knees, proceeding to place my dick inside of her mouth.

Maybe that was what I needed to take my mind off, of Zonnique. I felt guilty as my eyes closed, visioning Zonnique on her knees.

"Shit," I moaned.

The warmth of Mercedez wet and closed jaws made me feel like I was about to dissolve into the wall. My toes curled and I knew it would only take a minute before I released myself into her mouth. Mercedez begin to spit out bubbles as she sped up the momentum, I couldn't hold it in any longer; I was about to blow. I balled my fist and tilted my head back as she sucked up every, last drop. Physically I had the feeling of temporary satisfaction, mentally my head was somewhere else. All I could think about was Zonnique when she got up off of her knees and kissed me on my chin, like she was leaving me satisfied. I got out of my clothes, climbing inside of the jacuzzi styled tub, as Mercedez sat across from me with bubbles up to her breast. Even though a wine glass was in hands reach, she'd rather drink straight out of the champagne bottle.

"How was work today?" She asked, taking a long gulp before sitting the bottle down to focus her eyes back on her cellphone.

"Work was work." I told her. "Speaking of that, I been thinking about opening up my own business. You know, like investing in something other than standard oil. I've been a financial advisor for years, why not open up a business like a credit union or a bank?"

Mercedez crackled, hard enough for champagne to spray out of her mouth. "Please tell me you're joking, True." She asked while picking the bottle back up, to take another sip.

"Why would I be joking? And what's wrong with you?" I

said, serious than a fucking heart attack.

"I'm sorry for laughing, but you're about to be a billionaire and you're thinking about opening up your own business? Why would you want to do some stupid shit like that? I mean It just wouldn't make sense to me to try to go open, up your own business, when the oil and energy company is where the money is at. A bank? Please, True; Your father has enough money to fill up an entire bank. Besides, it won't be half as successful than your father's company." She took another sip of the bottle.

As I got out of the tub, the temperature of the water had suddenly become cold.

"Damn you sound just like everybody else." I grabbed a towel to dry off, knotting it below my pelvis bone.

"And what the hell is that supposed to mean?" Mercedez spat with suds dripping off, of her body as she climbed out of the tub, not worrying about the wet trail she made all the way into our bedroom.

"I've been preparing to take over the family fortune since I was young and you seem to think that, that's all I was created to do in life? Like I can't do anything else? What about my dreams and aspirations? Why is it that everything I do has to be attached to my father's name?" I asked as I changed into a pair of boxers.

"Because you're a Blackwell and you're the only son of the Blackwell." She answered as if I was supposed to be happy. "This is what you've been preparing for and it's what you're supposed to do. I mean where is all of this coming from anyways? I've never even heard you talk about your dreams and aspirations in life. I mean, True, look around you. You're living like a damn king and pretty, soon you'll be running a kingdom! Dreams and aspirations are for folks who don't have nothing but a dream and a dollar to their name; that's why it's called dreams and aspirations!" Mercedez said with confidence as she changed into one of my oversized T-shirts and a skimpy thong, climbing in the bed next to me while texting on her phone.

I turned over and went to sleep, praying that Zonnique would enter my dreams.

Serpent

When I turned my phone on and saw that I had three miscalls from Zonnique, I tried returning her phone call; hearing the phone ring only once before ending the call. If she didn't hit me right back, I knew she had probably put Zion to bed then went to sleep herself. That was what I wanted her to do. When I'd left the mansion, I had spent some time at the casino. Since it was late, I would just give Zonnique some excuse about me having work overtime, and that it was why I wasn't able to get home.

If Mercedez wouldn't have been on that bullshit earlier that day, I would have made it on my side of town before it even got pitch black. I mean we ain't even get a chance to fuck. After she tripped out and told me she was pregnant, I had to get the fuck up out of there. As I pulled up at my Mama Joyce house, the sound of a bell from a text message coming through my phone, caused me to put the car in park, leaving the engine running as I sat in the car.

Mercedez: I know you already said that you didn't care to know what I was going to do about our baby but I just want to let you know that next week, I plan on going to the doctor to find out how far along I am, and that my mind isn't made up on rather I would get an abortion or not.

I read the text before quickly deleting it, facing the screen down on the dashboard. I should have known too strap up when I was fucking with her. It was only supposed to be a hit it and quit thing, now she was trying to convince me to be okay with the fact that she was having my baby, but I wasn't. That baby was going to ruin my life. It was going to ruin the family that I'd built with Zonnique. I wanted Mercedez to get an abortion because if Zonnique was to ever find out about it, she would never forgive me, and I couldn't kiss my little family goodbye.

I was at my mama Joyce's house because I needed to pick something up before I placed my plan into action. I took out a suitcase on wheels, rolling it onto the porch before using the house key my mama gave me when I was a teen. I unlocked the door to let myself in the small apartment. I wanted to be as quiet as possible because the last thing I needed was to wake mama Joyce up. I didn't have time to hear her interrogation of questions, asking me shit, because she was the only person I couldn't lie to.

I walked into my bedroom and could hear all, of my snakes in their tanks hissing. I had to visit my mother's house frequently to check on them and it was time for their feeding. I fed each snake individually, dropping a white, mice in each of the snake's mouths. I had over a dozen snakes closed off in their own glass tank. I housed three anacondas, three vipers, three cobras, and two boas. My favorite kind of snake of all time, was my adult male reticulated python. I'd gotten him when he was just a baby, but he weighed over two hundred pounds and was about thirteen feet long. He was one inch away from being too big for me to keep in my care and pretty, soon it would take two people to hold him. He was outgrowing my room and I knew it was time for me to let him go.

I went over to his tank and slid the glass door halfway, open; it was just enough room just for me to reach my hand in so that I could get to him. When he tried to bite me with his fangs, I moved my hand back just in time; that bite would have stung. He was grumpy because I hadn't fed him in a little over a week. I adjusted my hand through the glove, before sliding the glass back to his boxed off enclosure. I held on to my long hook tool, carefully using the tool to rub under the belly of the snake.

Over the years of me taking care of reptiles, I learned that snakes would give you respect as, long as you showed them the same.

The python lurked at me with piercing slit eyes, as it moved its neck and upper body out of the enclosure, I picked up the lower half of its body, guiding it into the oversize suitcase and zipping it up inside. I was just about to make it to the door before I heard my mother call out to me from the other room.

"Serpent? Is that you? Now what are you doing here at this time of night? I thought I told you to stop barging in without calling me!" Mama Joyce yelled from the comfort of her bed.

She said it was too much work trying to walk around with a cane, which was why she didn't get out of bed unless she had to. I rolled the suitcase to the door before going into her room to greet her. The room was dark, but I could still see her face from the blue light of the television.

"I was just stopping by to feed the snakes. You know I don't like waking you up to feed them because I know it's a lot for you to do. I also know you said it was my responsibility to keep em alive." I told her as I came over to her bedside.

"I swear you love them snakes more than your own mother." She said while reaching over to give me a kiss, before taking a sip of water from the glass on her nightstand.

"How's that caregiver working out for you?" I asked her as I raised the both of her feet up, placing a pillow under her feet; hoping it would help with the blood circulation in her legs.

"I liked it better when I didn't have one." She groaned. "All that young lady does is sit down and get all in my business while talking on her little smart phone. Doctors say if I can improve my mobility this year, we can get rid of the caregiver. Maybe I'll even be able to do the mother and son dance at you and Zonnique's wedding."

"You will be, mama, don't you worry about that." I told

her as I took the glass from her, sitting it back down on the nightstand.

She must have taken her medication before I got there because she was dozing back off to sleep. I cut the television off and locked up the house, before loading my python into my truck.

∞∞∞

The time on my cell was twelve midnight. I made it to the Blackwell's facility, taking the elevator all the way to the top floor. I went down the hall and into Cyrus' office, walking all the way to the back where it was a door to a small room. I opened the door and saw him sleeping on this pullout, queen sized bed like Mercedez had told me. I unzipped my carry on, allowing the snake to sway it's head out fully. The giant snake slithered onto the floor, up the foot of the bed post and under Cyrus's cover. I watched the mountainous hump in the sheets as the python traveled its way to Cyrus chest.

"You might not want to take another move. They say that snakes can sense the heartbeat of its prey. You move and my pet python would have no problem ending you. Snakes could smell the blood of fear. Mines haven't had a piece of meat in a week and it's ready to feed." I informed, turning the office lamp on so that I could see his face.

Cyrus had stopped snoring, blinking his eyes rapidly as the snake slithered its tongue in his face.

"Serpent, what do you want?" He asked with a voice barely over a whisper. "When you came to me in a time of need, I gave you a job to feed your family and you return the favor by trying to kill me?"

"Fuck this job and fuck your charity. What would you

know about family? You damn near gave up on your own family years ago. Cheating on your wife by having sex with a minor. You're a fuckin pedophile, Cyrus. Mama Joyce still won't admit that she saw you the night we came back from that camping trip, and the only reason you gave me this job was because I took an oath to stay away from True. Making me promise to go on with my daily life like him and I was never stepbrothers. It's a shame that True doesn't even know that his stepbrother works here. You got one son working on the top and another son at the bottom. Now tell me how the fuck you sleep at night?"

"Real good knowing I built an empire." Cyrus said keeping still, looking like a wrapped mummy with his hands glued still to his side. I could see the fear in his eyes as my slit eyed reptile got closer to comfort.

Hsssssssss. Hsssssss. Hssssss.

As the snake hissed with its split tongue it began to wrap around Cyrus's neck.

"Alright, Serpent! I'll give you whatever you want. You name it. Just don't let this snake kill me."

"Now you sound like you coming to your senses." I said, making a circle as I walked around the bed. "I want the rights to the company; your wife didn't raise no dummy. I want you to sign off on it on your will." I grimaced, giving him a look that could kill.

"I can't do that, Serpent, and you know it." He denied my request.

"Yes, you can, and you will, or else! Now where is it? Before I leave you here with my snake to become his next meal."

Cyrus slowly pointed to his desk where I retrieved the will in his top drawer. I brought the paper over to him, along with a ball point pen. He scratched True's name off, before scribbling mine along with his approved signature.

"There. I signed it and gave you what you want. Now get this snake from around me!" Cyrus demanded as the snake wrapped tighter around his neck.

"You know what?" I said while folding my arms. "I think I changed my mind. I'll just sit here and watch what happens."

"YOU TREACHEROUS SNAKE!" Cyrus yelled as the reptile striked him on the side of the neck with its sharp fangs.

The python coiled its body around Cyrus' neck, its yellows skin mimicking the material of leather. Cyrus' face turned the color of blue. I could hear him wheezing as he began kicking with his legs against the foot board. If only I would have told him that the more he tried to move, the harder the snake would squeeze. The Python's thick coils stayed curled around Cyrus's neck, until I heard Cyrus take his last breath. His eyes rolled towards the back of his head, where I could only see the white part. A thud sounded from Cyrus's head dropping back onto the pillow, as the snake released his hold. I pulled the cover back over his body to make it looked as though he was sleeping like a baby. Now that I had the rights to the company, I was officially a millionaire!

I stopped at the nearest bayou, letting my snake slither into the swampy waters. When I made it home, I got out of my clothes and took a shower. Feeling the effects of exhaustion, still, I went inside of Zion's room to see that he was sleeping with his thumb in his mouth. I walked into my bedroom to see Zonnique sitting up, sleep with her head against the headboard. She must've fell asleep while trying to study because her laptop was still open, sitting on her lap. All, of her textbooks and loose paper was covering up the entire bed. I moved everything out of the way by placing it on top of her vanity. I knew Zonnique was working her ass off and I couldn't wait to make her my wife.

I kissed her before I got into bed with her. I wanted to give her the wedding she had deserved and now that I would be taking over the company, I finally could give her just that.

I was up at four A.M, shirtless, with a pair of joggers on, doing a morning run around the nice neighborhood; all while trying to stay in a positive mode. I had been slacking on my sessions lately but because I had a lot of things on my mind, I was hoping that getting up to beat the morning sun could clear my head of distractions. I had managed to get some sleep, but I couldn't say that I was sleeping comfortably, because Zonnique was in my dreams. I didn't even want to wake up, but I thought getting up out of the bed could make me forget about her. I was wrong because she was still heavy on my mind.

As *Juice*, by Lizzo came through my wireless ear buds, I tried to keep up with the beat as I reached the top of the hill; doing ten sets of dumbbell squats until I begin feeling that good pain from the stretch, in my hamstrings. For my last mile I closed the session out by sprinting all the way back to the mansion. When I went back inside of the house sweaty, I decided to step into the shower and get ready for work. As I stepped out of the shower, my cell was showing that it was Mrs. Fiona calling. Since she had been working for the company for so long, she was the only one who came into work by five A.M. I knew it had to be an emergency because she had never called me while I was at home; something told me that it had something to do with my father.

"Hello, Mr. True, I'm calling about your father." She said sounding like she was crying. "I'm sorry to be the one to inform you, but Cyrus is dead. I just clocked in and found him in his bed. His attorney is here in the office, he needs you to come down here to go over some legal documents. Oh, I'm so sorry, Mr. True."

The long pause had told me that Miss. Fiona was waiting to hear my reaction. I didn't have one. No tears, no nothing. All my life I'd been preparing for that moment, and you couldn't cry over something you'd prepared yourself for.

During the meeting with Cyrus's lawyer, on behalf of his wishes, he was cremated after his body was sent to the morgue. I was able to keep my father's mansion, but I was surprised when the lawyer said that the business didn't belong to me; that it belonged to my stepbrother.

"Where were you yesterday evening?" I asked Serpent while combing my wavy hair with a wig brush, in the bathroom's mirror.

I knew he had worked overtime because when I woke up, I'd noticed I'd had a miss call from him. I wanted to have the conversation with him the previous night, but I didn't realize how tired I was when I came in from the adventure Zion and I had with True. It was already bad enough that I was bringing this conversation up with Serpent the morning of my exams, but because he worked so late, it was the only time I'd found it necessary to bring it up.

Silence filled the room. Serpent didn't respond because he was too busy brushing his hair with a wave brush and examining himself in the mirror. That still didn't stop me from getting straight to the point.

"I'm asking because yesterday Zion and I went up to your job to surprise you with a lunch date and to my surprise, you were already out." I said in a questionable tone, staring at Serpent's face through the reflection of the mirror.

Noticing the pitch in my tone, Serpent finished up in the mirror before leaning his back on the bathroom's counter. The way he folded his arms and sucked in his lips, told me he was uncomfortable with talking about the subject and I wanted to know why.

"I wish you would have called me ahead of time before you came up to the J; I would have told you that I went out to eat with one of my coworkers." He said before going back in the mirror to line up the thin mustache, that parted in two above his top lip.

"Serpent I called you about three times and your phone, was going straight to voicemail." I told him, wishing I would have saved this convo for another time because I was getting irritated and didn't want it to affect my test.

"My battery died." He shrugged.

His three worded answer wasn't a good enough of an explanation for my liking. Serpent wasn't supposed to have his phone on him while working outside on the plant, so I didn't understand how his phone could have been dead. And if was dead, how was he even able to call me last night, unless he'd found a charger? Then about the co-worker he mentioned, everybody knew that men didn't go out for lunch with just one co-worker; not unless it was a date that involved another woman.

I wasn't the type of woman to accuse someone of cheating, until I had some proof. I wanted to give Serpent the benefit of the doubt because he couldn't possibly be that damn stupid to cheat on me, right before we even got married.

"Good morning, mama! Good morning, daddy!" Zion came running into the bathroom with the biggest smile flashed across his face, jumping into my arms. He was the only person who could turn my day from bad to good.

"Good morning, Zion. Good job with getting yourself dressed this morning!" I applauded him, fixing the collar to his uniform shirt. I kissed him on the cheek as Serpent ruffled with Zion's curly hair on top of his tapered fade, causing Zion to focus his attention on Serpent.

"Daddy, me and mama saw the biggest helicopter of all time!"

"You did?" Serpent said as Zion continued, on with the story.

"Uh huh." He nodded with exaggeration. "I tried to stay up and wait on you pass my bedtime like mama had told me I could, but I guess I fell asleep." Zion pouted. "Do you think if I wait up for you tonight, you can read me a bedtime story? I like it when mama read to me, but sometimes I want you to read to me too."

"Depends on what time I get off tonight." Serpent told him. "I can't guarantee you any promises because my job usually keeps me in late, but I'll try to make it before your bedtime."

"Okay,"

The way Zion's eyes went from Serpent then directly on the floor, had told me he wanted more of his father's attention. Spending time with True was a reminder that Serpent was slacking, and it was showing all over our son's face.

"How about you go downstairs and eat breakfast while we still have time." I said, trying to cheer Zion up. "There's a bowl of Fruit Loops on the counter with your name on it. Mama have a big test that I have to pass today, so we got to get you to school on time."

Zion skipped out of the bathroom and headed downstairs as I went into the bedroom. Since I'd already picked my clothes out the night before, all I had to do was get dressed to go.

"Have you been looking at any of the wedding stuff?" Serpent asked as he put on his gear for work.

"I'm meeting up with the girls to go searching for wedding dresses later, on." I said. "That's another thing I wanted to talk to you about. Since Christmas is coming up, I've been thinking about my parents."

"What about your parents?" Serpent asked dryly as he

stepped into his boots, sitting on the lazy boy furniture to lace the strings up.

"I wanted to go to their house around the holidays and invite them over to our house. Since you'll be off for the holidays, I didn't want Zion to have to open his gifts with just us and Mama Joyce. What do you think about me introducing them to Zion? Maybe they would even like to be a part of the wedding." I noted.

Serpent seemed doubtful as he began scratching the back of his head, before talking with his hands.

"Zonnique, you know how I feel about your parents and I know how they feel about me, man. Your father never approved of our relationship so why would I even want him or your mother in our wedding. Why would I even want em in our house, eating at our dining room table, like we one big ass happy family or some shit? You could start back talking to em if you want to, but I'm not as forgiving as you." He spoke from the side of his mouth. "I don't even want them to meet Zion."

Even though Serpent was responding, I don't think he was listening. It was disappointing to know that Serpent wasn't too big on inviting them to our wedding, but it was more disappointing to know that he didn't want Zion meeting his grandparents.

"But that's my mother and father, Serpent!" I said with a croak in my throat.

My feelings must have really been triggered because I had tears running like a waterfall down my cheeks. If I could forgive my parents, I didn't understand why couldn't, he.

"Don't cry, Nique." He said, getting up to stand between my legs as he spoke to me softly. "I know how much this wedding means to you which is why I'm going to make sure it's over the top; a wedding met for a Queen, like what we've talked about before. But I don't want you stressing about the wedding like this. I promise everything is going to be alright."

I nodded in agreement. I wanted to believe him, but I didn't. Yes, I was stressed about the wedding on top off being stress with school, but I think somehow Serpent believed that throwing me this extravagant wedding would make me forget about my mother and father. I didn't care about having a big wedding, hell I would have been good with a guest list of one hundred people. All that really mattered to me was that I'd be surrounded with love, family and friends.

After Zion was done eating, I dropped him off at his school and was inside of the computer lab, waiting for word on rather I'd passed the test to become an ultrasound tech. The test had covered a multiple number of exams but once I passed, I would graduate then complete my clinical hours. I couldn't wait to work one on one with a patient, it was what I had been working hard for. I was nervous about the exam, being that I was the last one to finish but I was confident enough to know that I'd passed.

When Professor Daniel's finished getting everybody's scores in, he called student's one by one into his office, handing every passing student a pair of official medical scrubs. I knew I would be called last since I was the last one to finish my exam.

"Zonnique Jones." Professor called out.

I couldn't get out of my desk because my eyes were still closed; I would be taking one of the most important walks to my future. With sweaty palms, I took a deep breath and exhaled.

Here goes nothing.

"You passed." He said, as he handed me a pair of medical scrubs, with my name stitched above the pocket.

I blew out a breath of relief and could have cried tears of joy. I had passed the exam with flying colors and was officially an ultrasound tech. Now that everyone had received their scores, I was waiting on him to finish his announcement.

"Ladies and Gents, as you all know there will be only be one finalist that gets the chance to be my intern, with a guaranteed position as a prenatal ultrasound technician at my family practice. I have that name of that intern posted outside this door and when class ends, you all can be dismissed. Good luck to everyone and may the best one win."

As the bell rung, the entire body of class portrayed a stampede while I was still in my seat, trying to call Serpent to tell him that I'd passed my exam. When the phone went to voicemail, I texted him instead. Still high off, of my exam as I walked out of class, I had almost forgot about checking the paper that Professor Daniel's posted. I wasn't surprised at all that the crowd of students had died down. I reassured myself that I wouldn't be upset, if I didn't make the finalist for the internship either. Passing my exams was good enough of an accomplishment for me. Still. My eyes couldn't help but to skim the sheet of paper. I held my breath before letting it go. Centered in italic font, black and bold print, was the name **_Zonnique Jones_**.

"Congratulations, Zonnique. Your father should be proud of you." Professor Daniel's said, shaking my hand as I cried.

"Thank you so much for believing in me Professor; you don't know how much this means to me, seriously."

"You just make sure to meet me at my family practice." He said clearing his throat and going back into the lab.

Since it was the beginning of the Christmas break, I'd dropped Zion off at Mama Joyce house for a few days, making my way to David's Bridal where Myrah and Brooke was waiting for me with a bottle of bubbly.

"You are now looking at the next prenatal ultrasound tech. Ayeeeeee!" I said twerking before Brooke, Myrah and I hurdled around for a three-person hug.

"Ahhhhh! Congratulations!" Myrah said as she handed me a champagne glass.

"This calls for a celebration!" Brooke cheered as she popped the cork off a bottle of champagne, shaking it as the foam of bubbles went everywhere. After she filled all three of our glasses, we clinked them together before sipping in unity.

"Now let's find you a dress, girl!"

The wedding was approaching towards the end of the month and Serpent told me that it was no limit when it came to finding a dress. While Brooke and Myrah was sitting on the mini sectional waiting for my arrival, I was inside of the dressing room getting fitted for my first gown of choice; a mermaid fitted gown with beading around the waistline and a heart shape neckline, designed by Vera Wang. Ten thousand dollars was the price. The off white, cream colored material, felt good against my skin. They said that you could feel it in your spirit when it was the dress and since I wasn't in front of a mirror, I was ready to walk down the runway and see the dress for myself.

When the female store associate zipped my dress up in the back, adding a netted lace veil with a long train, she handed me a bouquet of white roses and said, "Here comes the bride, ladies."

I could hear a gasp, followed by a couple of *Ohhhh's* and *Ahhhhh's*. Myrah and Brooke had stood on their feet as if they were ready to give me a standing ovation, only they were dabbing the corners of their eyes with balls of tissue. Even though I could barely see through the netting of the veil as I one two stepped down the runway, the sound of my heels lightly clanking against the wood, made everything feel so surreal. I didn't open my eyes until I felt the veil being lifted away from my face. As I stared at my reflection in the head to toe mirror, I was surprised. I wasn't feeling that tingly feeling that every bride described, and I didn't know why.

"You look like the prettiest bride I've ever seen." Brooke said as Myrah handed her a digital camera, wanting to take a picture of the moment.

Myrah stepped onto the runway and said, "You've been waiting on this moment since you were pregnant with Zion and now it's finally here! Can you believe you're about to be Mrs. McKinney?"

When Brooke snapped the picture, I gave the camera a half smile, lifting my hand up to see the ring in the light.

No. I couldn't believe it.

I thought finding out that Cyrus was dead would make me feel better, but it only meant that I was free of one issue. Being pregnant had my body feeling like a complete train wreck. Aside from the morning sickness, I knew I was getting further along in my pregnancy because I was starting to feel flutters in my stomach.

True was down at the morgue picking up Cyrus ashes. It had been two weeks since I had heard from Serpent and I was tired of him playing games, but I couldn't focus on him because I had an appointment with my OBGYN, and I had my baby to think about. Thankful that the weather had become colder towards the end of December, I had a whole excuse to cover up my stomach that was starting to look as if I was bloated. I didn't even feel up to dressing all cute, I only wanted to get in and out of the doctor's office, so fashion wasn't my main priority. When I confirmed that I was coming to my ultrasound appointment over the phone, I called for a car to pick me up out front. A Yeezy hoodie over my head with over-sized Dolce and Gabbanna shades covering half my face, had told the chauffeur that I wasn't in the mood to be fucked with.

As I walked into the doctor's office scribbling my name on the sign in sheet at the front desk, I handed the receptionist my I.D and insurance card. When she was done making a copy of my information, I groaned as she handed me back my identification cards and a thick ass packet that I didn't even feel like filling out. I sat in the middle of two empty chairs because I didn't feel like sitting next to anyone else. As I was writing, I notice a little girl come in with a pair of glittery Twinkle toed shoes. Her tan skin and baby afro, was pulled back, tied down with a pink ribbon. She was smiling as she held on to her mother and father's hand, right before her father picked her up and placed her in a seat between him and the mother. The little girl simpered. She had to be about five years old. She reminded me of myself when I was that age. I wish I could tell her to hold on to her parents a little tighter because she never knew when she was going to lose them.

Scarlett was my mother's name, but most people called her Apples. She could be picked first from out of the bunch. With fair skin, eyes the color of limes and strawberry blonde hair, daddy use to say she favored one of them cabbage patch dolls the way her beauty marks connect the dots across her face. Everybody would tell me that I was my mother's twin, but I was attached to my daddy's hip. Daddy would be dressed in his camouflage uniform with his luggage in hand. He would sit me on his lap and call me his Little Red, saying I was the prettiest girl in the whole wide world and to never forget it. I would cry and just hug him. I knew he was about to leave me, and I didn't know when I would see him again. Daddy was a soldier. He wore his uniform proudly, that was how he and mother met. Mama was a lead singer in a group and was on stage singing the national anthem to the soldiers. When daddy saw her, he said it was like she sung her way through his heart. That's how they ended up having me.

When daddy would be away fighting for the country, my uncle Sedan would come over to our house and even bring his son, my big cousin Bugatti, along with him to play with me sometimes. Uncle Sedan would even spend the night with me and my mother. I would ask mother why Uncle Sedan was spending so much time at our house, she would say daddy was away in the army and a lot of things like the washer and dryer machine was broken, and that my uncle Sedan was the only person she could call to come fix it. I didn't understand how he was fixing things around the house because I never even saw my uncle Sedan with a toolbox. When I would knock on my parent's door, my Mama would tell me to go in my room or go outside in the back yard to play, while uncle Sedan was in the house trying to work.

I did what I was told and went outside in the front yard; I was swinging on the swing my daddy built for me and hung onto our Japanese plum tree. When I saw my daddy getting off the bus, I was so happy to see him. I knew I could get in trouble for, running out of the yard, across the street and into my daddy's arms but I missed my daddy so much, all I could do was just hug him.

"Hey, my pretty red," Is how he would say it, picking me up, giving me a million and one kisses while walking towards the house.

"Where's your mother and what are you doing outside by yourself?" He asked, as I tried on his army hat.

"Mama said I could play outside while uncle Sedan is working in the house."

Then that's when my daddy's whole mood changed; His face turned red hot. With me in his arms, he stormed inside of the house and kicked down the bedroom door with his boot. The loud commotion caused my mother to scream. She was on top of uncle Sedan as she grabbed the comforter, pulling it over her body. Daddy threw me down and I hid under a chair, as he and my uncle began tousling.

"Stop it before you kill him!" My mother told my father as he held uncle Sedan down in a choke hold.

I didn't even think he heard my mother until she went inside of the closet, coming back out with a big black gun, pointing it at the back of my daddy's head. I was crying while daddy slowly put his hands up. Uncle Sedan stood up, asking my mother if she was okay to be left with my daddy by herself. My mother just told my uncle Sedan that he needed to leave while he still could. I was about to get up from under the chair, when my mother and father began wrestling for the gun. I ducked back under the chair and covered my eyes, hoping the fight would soon be over. I didn't open my eyes until I heard the sound of a loud blast, followed by my mother placing her hands over her stomach frantically, looking at the color of red on her hands. I got up and ran over to my mother, kneeling and crying as I tried to wake her up, but she wouldn't even open her eyes. It was like she had fallen sound to sleep; something told me she was gone.

"I'm so sorry pretty little red," Was the last thing my father said before he jammed the barrel of the gun under his chin, turning the gun on himself. That was the day my world had been torn apart.

"Mercedez Taylor," The woman holding a clipboard, dressed down in blue scrubs, called out to me.

I got up from my seat in the waiting area taking my shades off, using them as a headband to push the hair back from in front of my face. I read the name Zonnique, on the woman's name badge. She had a pretty name and for a dark, skinned girl with hair longer than mine, she was also pretty. As she walked me to the patient's room, she asked, "Are you in any pain or just emotional?"

I knew she had to be new because she was still setting the room up with her ultrasound equipment.

"I'm just Emotional as shit. Like, I can't believe I even got myself in this situation." I told her as I sat on the medical exam table.

"It happens to the best of us. Just know that you're not alone." She said to me, patting me like a friend on the back.

"Well it wasn't supposed to happen to me." I told her as I rolled my eyes, crossing my arms with a snooted nose. She didn't respond back, maybe because she thought I sounded like one of them judgmental girls; I was just saying.

As she smiled, I could tell that she was annoyed with my arrogance, handing me one of them blue paper sheets to tuck into the inside of my pants before I laid down on my back.

"I'm going to have you pull your shirt up; the goal is to protect your clothing from the gel. You can go ahead and undo your pants and tuck the sheet around the hip line for me."

I nodded as I followed instructions. Since it was my first time experiencing it, she made me feel comfortable as she explained everything to me.

"This is some warm gel; I'm going to put this on your belly." She said as she squeezed from the tube of blue gel. "This helps the ultrasound waves go in, so we can get a clear picture of the baby." She explained as she stood up, pressing some buttons while we both watched the dark tinted gray screen.

It felt weird as she pressed the probe against my stomach.

"So, we're zeroing in on the baby's head; you can see the finger's right there. The baby's heart is beating just fine. We'll zoom up, so I can get a tracing of the heart." She said as she took pictures of what was on the screen. "Judging by the fetal size and length of the baby, you are exactly nine weeks."

Nine weeks. I thought, wishing Serpent was sitting next to me and we were both watching our baby on the screen together as a family. Then I thought about True and how all, of it would break his heart.

"You may zip your pants back up." The technician said as she wiped the gel off of me, cutting back on the light before handing me my pictures of the ultrasound.

"Thank you, and I didn't mean it like that when I said that things like this doesn't happen to me." When I sat up, she stood there and listened to me. "What I meant to say was, I have been messing around with my baby daddy for a year and even though he doesn't want the baby, I don't even much know what I should do. I guess I shouldn't want the baby either, being that I have a fiancé."

I didn't know why I was talking to the woman but because she didn't know me from a crack in the wall, it didn't feel bad to talk to her.

"Have you told either one of them the truth?" She asked, taking her time as she wiped her equipment down with a sanitation cloth. Talking to me as if she felt sorry for me.

"My fiancé doesn't know, but I've told my baby daddy. I even told him that I was going to the doctor's office. Just the other day, I sent him a text but I haven't heard from him since."

"I can't believe some men." She said, in a disappointing look.

My phone binged in between my legs, showing it was a text message from Serpent.

"Speaking of the devil." I told her as I read the message to myself. "The freakin nerve of him. I said. Read what he'd sent me."

I gave her my phone as she read it out loud.

Tell me how many weeks you is so I can know how much I need to pay for the abortion. Your mind made up yet?

"And how long have you been knowing him?" The technician asked me, as she still held on to my phone.

"I knew of him from this high school we use to both go to, people use to call him Snake. He used to be short but now he's gotten fine. Why do you ask? Do you know him or something?"

"No. Just curious." She said, giving me back my phone.

"What was his reaction when you first told him you were pregnant?" She asked.

"He started talking about how he wouldn't claim my baby if I had it because he didn't know how he would go home and tell his fiancé, and that he already has his family."

"Well if you knew that, then why would you be a hoe and fuck a nigga who already has a family?"

"What did you just say to me?" I asked.

"Alright, Mercedez." My gynecologist, Dr. Daniels, walked in as the technician walked out.

"Here is your prescription, to get started on your prenatal care. I'm sure you've already met my new hire, Zonnique."

"I met her," I said still thinking about the woman's rude comment. "Thanks for the prescription, and I'll be sure to schedule my next appointment upfront." I told Dr. Daniels before leaving the patient room.

"Walk me through what the text message said one more time; are you for sure that was Serpent who texted that patient, Zonnique?" Brooke's voice asked through the car's blue tooth speaker.

With my hands on the steering wheel, I was sucking my lips in and shaking my head as I tried to process the fact that Serpent was cheating on me. *Nine weeks pregnant? We're supposed to be a family and this nigga go out and get another bitch pregnant?! So last Christmas while me and his son was at his mama house, he was fucking another bitch?*

I didn't even need to screenshot it because I'd saw what I saw and If Serpent thought I was about to wait at home for his phone call, he had another thing coming. I ended the conversation with Brooke. Driving out of my workplace, I quickly glanced in the rearview mirror at my wedding dress hanging up, covered in the clear packaging. I adjusted the mirror. I didn't even want to think about the wedding at that moment.

As my fingers went to his number, ready to dial, I changed my mind on calling to ask him about it. Throwing my phone into the back seat, I tried swallowing the painful lump in my throat, memorizing the text message inside of my head. Serpent couldn't deny it because it was most definitely his name and number. With my hands controlling the steering wheel, I didn't even know how I was driving because my focus was far from the road.

Serpent had promised to be mines, truly and forever and he goes out and does this? After all he promised me; His family? I just feel so disrespected.

I could barely even see from the tears that were making my vision blurry, causing me to shake the tears from my lids, as I tried focusing on driving. I knew I probably should've been going home but Serpent had me messed up if he thought I was going to wait. So, there I was, acting like one of them scorned women because I was headed up to his job. Every girl is allowed to act crazy at least once, and I had questions that needed answers.

When I made it to the facility, I didn't have time to park into the garage. I parked in the limited parking spots, in front of the library; it was urgent. I got out of the car, slamming the door as I walked into the building towards the security booth. When I asked for a cheating ass McKinney, I was surprised when they informed me that he worked in the office. Bewildered about the promotion at his job, I caught the elevator up to the floor where his receptionist, Miss Fiona, showed me to his big office.

"Serpent?" I asked as Miss Fiona closed the office door behind me.

The old lady left us to our privacy. His feet were up; he pulled at a Cuban cigar, blowing a cloud of smoke in my face.

"What brings you here, Zonnique? Did you come all the way up here to tell me about your first day at your new job?" Serpent asked as he got comfortable in the executive chair, smiling with this dumb grin on his face.

"You damn right I came up here to tell you about my job." I said sweetly, forcing a smile on my face. "But first I wanted to ask you something." I said in a questioning tone reaching over the desk, getting close, up on his face.

"What did you need to ask me, baby?" He said sexually, ashing his cigar into the gold ashtray. Waiting for what I was going to do next, he stuck the cigar back into his mouth.

Whop!

My open hand found the side of his face.

"When were you going to tell me that you were fucking somebody else?!" I shouted, as Serpent touched the side of his lip, suddenly angry from seeing a speck of blood on his finger.

"I'm not fucking nobody else but you, Nique. CHILL!" He looked like he wanted to hit me as he stared at me quietly. Only shaking his head like he deserved it, puffing back on his cigar.

"You really just gone sit up here and lie to me in my face, Serpent? I just want you to tell me if it's true?" I asked as the desk stood in between us.

To witness Serpent's reaction when he was confronted with the truth, caused anger to build up inside of me. As I leaned my butt against the desk, all I could do is shake my head. I was fuming but I wasn't about to cry. He didn't deserve to see me hurting like that.

"Damn don't do that, Queen." Serpent got up and walked towards me. "Do you really want to know the truth? Alright. You're right. I was fucking somebody else, but it was nothing serious, you gotta believe me. You know the only person I want to be with is you."

"Serpent do you need to tell me anything else?" I said, still trying to give him a chance because at that moment, it sounded like he was just telling me what I wanted to hear.

"Naw man, that's it; I promise. Why do you ask?"

"You forgot to mention that she's nine weeks pregnant." I said, feeling like he was pushing a dagger deeper into my heart.

"How do you? Mannnnnnnnn," He thought about it as he dragged. "That baby might not even be mines!"

"How could you, Serpent?" I pushed him out of my way. "Were you even thinking about Zion and, I? Your family! Or was you thinking with your other head?" I asked.

"Baby, it wasn't even like that." Serpent tried to come back to kiss me, but I moved out of the way, causing him to almost fall.

"Come on, Nique. Baby look around! Can't you see I did all of this for our family?" He asked, dusting himself off as he stood in front of the floor to ceiling window. He took another cigar out of the pocket of his shirt. "We're fuckin millionaires now. We don't ever have to worry about shit, can't you see. I can give you the dream wedding you always wanted!"

"Serpent the wedding is off." I said, slipping off my ring and placing it on the desk. "Yes, money mattered but you know I never cared about being rich. The dream wedding you wanted to spoil me with, is sounding more like yours. When you come home, don't expect me to wait up for you." I said, walking out of his office.

"Nique! Nique!" Serpent called out, stepping out into the hallway. "Just remember I did all of this for you. You know I love you right?"

I turned around for just a second. "Oh really? Because it seems to me that you only love yourself." I said, before getting onto the elevator.

I wished he would have chased after me, but it honestly wouldn't have been no good. No matter how much making up Serpent tried to do, he'd never be able to undo what was already been done, I thought as I pressed the button to the first floor of the lobby. Just to think we would be spending Christmas together. Realizing that the ring was no longer on my finger when the elevator doors closed shut, I took that moment to cry.

A thousand-dollar china, crystal urn sat on my desk, filled with Cyrus's ashes. After learning that his legacy had belong to my stepbrother, Serpent, he'd left a lot of questions unanswered. I saw it as a sign. It was time I started making my own moves. I was just about finished opening a few business accounts for the day and was, in need of a break from the computer; maybe even from the office.

I went inside of my side drawer, taking out the book that Zonnique had given me. I only read halfway through the book *The Upper Room* by Mary Monroe but the whole time I was reading, I couldn't concentrate on the words on the pages because I was thinking about her again. When the checkout receipt slipped out of one of the pages showing that the book was due to be turned back in that day, I locked up my office to go down to the first floor of the lobby. Besides a few people sitting at the computers, the library was empty. I walked all the way into the back of the library, passing up the urban fiction bookshelves before I dropped the book into the drop off box.

I walked through one of the aisles when I saw Zonnique sitting on a mini sofa, in the corner of a reading nook. I knew she probably had just gotten out of school or work because she had on scrubs, with prescription glasses that made her look like a sexy kitten. I thought maybe something was wrong with her because she wasn't reading a book or anything. She was just sitting back in the chair, arms folded, and shoulders slumped, while rubbing her ring finger. I didn't know if she felt like being bothered or not, but I wasn't about to leave without making sure.

"*Pssssssst,* Zonnique." I whispered, feeling like I was back in junior high.

I could see the look of relief on her face when she noticed that it was me who was trying to get her attention. She tried to muster a smile, raising her glasses up to wipe under her liquid gold, eyes. I wanted to see if she was okay, so I walked up to her.

"Tell me what's wrong." I said, helping her out of the chair, noticing the redness in her eyes.

I didn't know if she had allergies because of the pollen season or if she was really crying, until I slid her prescription glasses off, of her face. She didn't say anything as I did. Her eyes were red, puffy and watery like she had been crying all day. When I tried to make eye contact with her, she hesitated by turning her head, tucking her baby hair behind her ear.

Damn I wish I could suck on her bottom lips!

Instead I took her by the chin, speaking in a low deep tone into her ear.

"You can tell me what's wrong and I swear I won't judge." Our lips were an inch away from touching.

She took in a deep breath through her nose, blowing air back out of her mouth as she looked at me.

"I'm supposed to be happy that I've started my first day at my job as an ultrasound technician, but now I just feel so stupid. The patient I was giving a sonogram to turned out to be a woman who's nine weeks pregnant by my fiancé. On top of that, he's gotten some promotion that he didn't even tell me about, where he moved into this big ass office; talking with enough air to fill up his head."

Is she talking about Serpent? Could she be Serpent's fiancé? I thought. He was the only person who'd gotten promoted up to office. I thought maybe I should just ask her, but I was scared of her reply. I even thought about letting her just walk away, but a part of me thought maybe I'd developed feelings for her, and I couldn't just let her walk away.

"Don't you work in the office, True?" Zonnique asked, out of the blue.

"SHHHHHHH," An older white woman, that was looking at us through a gap of books on the shelf, placed her finger over her mouth. Zonnique then tried to whisper, with tears that left an ashy trail down her cheeks.

"I'm supposed to be getting married and planning a wedding, right in time for Christmas. I'm not supposed to be worrying about the fact that my fiancé has a baby on the way. I even gave him a chance to tell me the truth and he still tried to deny that the baby is his. He couldn't even look me in the eye and tell me the whole truth." She mumbled, with brown eyes that traced the floor.

I took her by the hand and said, "I want you to come with me."

When we walked up the employee stairs and made it to my helicopter, Zonnique begin shaking her head while pulling away.

"Uh uh, True. What the hell?" She placed her hands on her hips.

"What." I asked.

Where do you think you're taking me in that thing and how do I know I can trust you with my life?"

I grinned and took out my license that showed that I was a qualified pilot. "You can trust me, Zonnique." I said as she took the card and examined the front and the back, before handing it back to me.

"Okay, but I must kind of like you because I don't like heights." She admitted as she took a hold of my hand.

"Don't worry about it, I got you." I told her, while opening the door and helping her in, wishing that she would also trust me with her heart.

As I got into the pilot's seat, I made sure we were both buckled in before lifting the controller stick, programming the helicopter on auto pilot. I wanted to focus my attention on her. Zonnique was looking out of the window as we soared through the clouds and precipitation.

"How's Zion doing?"

She looked at me like she was surprised that I'd even asked about him. "He's doing good, spending time with his grandmother for the holidays."

I nodded at her response.

We flew the rest of the way in silence. I knew I had a lot on my mind as well as herself. I was thinking about my deceased father; I wanted to know what would happen to the company, but it was out of my hands. I put my thoughts on the back burner as we landed on a private island in Texas, called Turtle's Bayou; just north of Corpus Christi. The island stretched to 48 acres of sandy land and lake.

"Why is this place so beautiful?" Zonnique asked in awe, looking at the breathtaking scenery.

"This is the only place in Texas that I know is still warm in the winter."

I had never taken Mercedez out there. If it wasn't a fancy five-star restaurant or exclusive establishment, she wouldn't approve of it. Something told me that Zonnique would appreciate the seclusion just as much as I did. I'd found about this place back when I was looking for a location I could meditate at. If

Zonnique needed some head space, it was definitely the right place for it.

When I opened the door to the helicopter, I took Zonnique's hand as she started to get out.

"You might want to leave your shoes in the helicopter, unless you want to track sand in them." I told her as I took my shoes off and left them on the seat.

She used each foot to take off each of her crocs, leaving them on the floor of the helicopter. I grabbed a cooler that I kept in the back with my lunch inside. I'd originally planned on going out there by myself, but I'd always packed enough food for two, just in case I stayed out there longer. Along with the cooler, I grabbed a throw blanket that I kept, tucked under the seat. As Zonnique and I walked together on the beach we picked a spot near the shore, close enough to feel the waves of the water splashing onto our feet. I spread out the blanket and Zonnique took a seat. I went inside of the mini cooler, taking out a California turkey wrap that was sliced into two. Zonnique took out a plastic container that had a section of fruit, yogurt, cheese and crackers. I took out a flannel of alcohol that was in the cooler, pouring Zonnique a cup of brown. Normally I only drank on occasions, but I felt like this was an exception. If anybody deserved a drink, the both of us did.

We ate our lunch in peace enjoying the view of the beach, while hearing the currents sway in the water. When I was done eating, I took some bread that I'd had left over from my wrap, tearing it into crumbs while feeding the seagulls that flocked around us.

"What do you do when you're out here by yourself?" Zonnique asked as she took a sip of the drink, breaking a cracker into half while feeding the seagulls with me.

"If I tell you, that means you have to do it with me." I said, standing up to unbutton my clothes.

Zonnique must've gotten the wrong idea as she gave me this look with one of her eyebrows raised, checking out my athletic physique while kissing the rim of her drink slowly.

"What kind of woman do you think I am?"

"Relax woman." I told her while stepping out of the legs of my pants. "I'm just stripping down to go for a swim." She looked relieved, but she still didn't bulge.

"I don't even have a bathing suit to get in," She said as she finished drinking her drink.

"When you make up your mind, you're more than welcome to join me." I told her as I made a run towards the lake, dunking myself into the cold water.

The sensation of the down temperature had shot up my body as I swam back up to the surface, clearing the water from my nose. I could see Zonnique standing up at the shore as she yelled.

"Can I have some privacy, please!" I smiled, turning around so she could get out of her clothes.

When I turned back around, Zonnique was bare in her skin. I admired her hourglass figure and the tiger stripes on each side of her thighs. As she dipped her toe into the water, she shivered, before holding her nose and submerging her body into the water. When she came up for air, she cupped her fingers to pull all of her hair back. She swam to me and I held on to her hips as we became face to face. Zonnique locked her legs around me, her arms hugged the back of my neck. As I balanced the circumference of her ass in my hands, I couldn't help but to be brick hard. This woman was gorgeous to me. We were surrounded by the deep blue waters as the waves pushed our warm bodies, closer and closer to each other; Zonnique stared at me.

"What are you thinking about?" She asked, her hair wet

and wavy.

"How good it feels to be the only two people on this island."

It was driving me crazy! If I was going to steal a kiss from her, the time would be then. With my eyes closed, I went forward with my lips. I was kissing her slowly, paying extra attention to her bottom lip, that had been asking to get sucked on ever since the first day I'd met her. When we both opened our eyes, I knew that she could feel my growing inches.

"I've been waiting to have the chance to kiss them big lips." I said.

We were still face to face in the water when Zonnique suddenly dipped her head under water. As I begin to look for her, she found my shaft with her mouth. I didn't even know it was possible to give head under the water, but she proved me wrong. Her pillowed lips felt like heaven on my dick. Not wanting her to drown I picked her up, sucking on her neck as we barely made it to the bank of the shore.

"Oh, my goodness, True." I could see Zonnique arch her back, my touch made her dig her fingers into the wet sand.

As I trailed my tongue around each of her chocolate nipples, I left a slimy trail down to her navel, all the way to the middle of her inner cotton candy center. I allowed her hands to wrap around my head as my two teeth played around with her clit. As she moaned, I could taste her sticky sap on my lips.

"Fuck me, True." Zonnique begged in a low tone.

"You sure you about that life?" I asked her.

The way she licked her lips her told me she was. As I reached for my pants that were off to the side, I took the extra-large magnum out of my wallet. I tore the packaging, rolling the condom onto my shaft. I looked down at her smoking hot body, she grunted as I maneuvered my inches inside of her. With my muscles flexed, I guided my curved steel, as we rocked our hips like we were making love on a boat.

When Zonnique let out a sex cry, I stopped, thinking I was going to rough until she whimpered, "Please just fuck me, True. Fuck me." She begged, like she needed my dick in her life.

With the determination to give her the best pleasure that I could give, I pinned her legs behind her head, making her pussy submit to my dick. I deep fucked her carefully, taken aback when a gush of water trickled down her legs. Zonnique was squirting! I knew she had never squirted before, because she looked surprised that her body was even capable of such a thing. I placed my head on one side of her shoulder, still holding her legs back as I looked at her; I needed to see her face. She looked like a mermaid as the water came onto the shore, rising up to our bodies. My dick felt like it was swimming in her pussy.

"Oh True," She whined. "I'm cumming!"

Those were the words that made me ejaculate into the tip of the condom. As Zonnique laid on top of my chest, we let the water from the waves wash the sex off, while watching the panoramic view of the lake.

After True flew me back to the facility, all different types of mixed emotions were going through my mind as we were still in the helicopter, letting our clothes air dry on to our skin, while I sat in the middle of his lap. The way he wrinkled his nose when he looked down at his watch, had told me that he didn't want to leave m but he needed to get back to work. I understood. Besides, I had a spa day with the girls and True's blanket had already warmed me up.

"You want me to walk you to your car?" He asked, his thumb rubbing my lip as we stood on the rooftop.

"No, I think you've done enough." I flirted with him, pinning my hair up with a single bobby pin I'd found at the bottom of my purse. True's eyes squinted and his top lip slightly puckered when he smiled; which told me he'd caught on to my dirty joke.

"I'll be fine to walk to my car. I parked close in front of the library anyways." I said, not wanting to do the walk of shame with True, being that we'd had sex and I was leaving the same workplace he shared with Serpent.

I didn't know if I should've been embarrassed or turned on at the fact that True had the talent and ability to make me squirt. That was something Serpent had tried so many times to make me do, yet I never could for him. As True and I walked inside of the building, I was trying to figure out how he knew my body better than Serpent did, when we'd only had sex just once. I'd quickly come to the conclusion, that God had blessed him with some hypnotizing dick, and I needed to stop overthinking about him, before I accidentally caught feelings.

"I have to go, True." I told him as we stood on the employee's stairway.

When he tried to hug me, I could smell the scent of his Tom Ford cologne as I placed my hands up on his chest, turning away from him before forcing myself to finally say goodbye.

"Zonnique,"

Ugh...why did his sexy ass have to say my name like that? True sounded confused as I made an exit down the stairs and into the parking lot in front of the library, but I wasn't confused about it at all. Maybe he was like every other man and only wanted the same thing; I tried to tell myself, as I got into my car.

We had sex and that was that. Nothing more and nothing less.

When I made it home, I took a shower, changing into a casual outfit. I was glad to have a reason to get back out of the house because I damn sure wasn't trying to wait for Serpent at home. I was on on my way to a well needed trio date with Brooke and Myrah, at this spa called the Pink Oasis. Myrah and Brooke had booked me an early wedding present and even though I had called the wedding off, it was no point of canceling a day with my girls. We needed to catch up anyways.

As the three of us, finished getting a relaxing rub down in an exfoliating oil on the mas-sue table, we each sat in massage chairs with fresh cucumber slices over our eyes, and a chunky avocado mask covering our faces. We began to talk as our mani and pedi's dried.

"Is the wedding really off, Nique?" Myrah asked.

"After I tell ya'll what I did, you would think so." I said. "I'm glad that we were able to link up, so I can tell ya'll what happened earlier, but you two have to make a promise not to judge me." I laid my head back on the vibrating head rest.

"Please don't tell me that you checked into a hotel and had a three some with two women, or had a train ran on you, that involved two men!" Brooke joked with her sarcastic, always horny ass.

"Not exactly." I said. "I can't believe I'm about to tell ya'll this. After I called off the wedding with Serpent, I ended up going to the library; where I ran into this guy from his job name, True. We had sex on a private island, and I don't even know how to feel about it."

"Trueeee?" They both pronounced his name in unison.

"True sounds cute." Myrah said.

"True sounds like he's, fine as hell!" Voiced Brooke. "Bout time you played a you on you shidddddd. Serpent had a whole baby on you, girl. I wouldn't feel bad about a mother fuckin thang!" I could hear Myrah clapping her hands together, in agreement.

"But wait, what do you mean by, you don't know how to feel about it? Myrah asked. "Was the sex not good or something?"

"You see, that's the thing," I told them. "The sex was great, too damn great if you ask me! True even made me squirt and I've never done that before with Serpent."

"He made you squirt, on the, beach? Do tell more!" Brooke freaky ass shouted in the quiet spa, sitting up as one of her cold cucumbers, landed on my thigh causing me to take the two cucumbers from off, of my eyes.

"Yes ya'll. This man made me squirt my insides out! But it was the way he held me afterwards. Like he freakin knew what I needed." I said with my eyes closed, only to picture his face behind my eyelids.

"Well, sounds like you had a lot of fun to me." Brooke leaned up as she took the cucumber from her eye and stuck it inside of her mouth. "True sounds like the kind of guy you truly need. Just take it slow with him because what you don't want to do, is gain feelings for True and he doesn't feel the same way back."

Who said I had feelings for him?

"And whatever you decide to do with Serpent, just know that we're still going to support you no matter what." Myrah said. "We just want to truly see you happy, because after all, that's all that matters at the end of the day."

"I agree." I told them as we finished getting pampered at the spa.

Serpent

I got up from the couch, trying to massage the crook in my neck. After I had come home from work the previous night, I was surprised when Zonnique kicked me out of our bed, throwing me a pillow and sending me to the doghouse in our living room. I knew she was still mad about the situation and I knew I'd fucked up when she called the wedding off, but damn! I didn't think it would get this far.

As I went into our kitchen, taking the warm breakfast off the hot skillet, I was trying to do whatever I needed to do to get back in her good graces. I wanted to start the weekend off right by making it up to her, because there was no way I could risk losing her and my family. I walked up the stairs with a tray of pancakes, sausage and eggs. You could never go wrong when it came to a chick who loved food.

"Rise and Shine, beautiful." I said while walking into the bedroom, holding the tray as I stood in front of the bed. Zonnique was up reading one of her urban fiction books but still in bed, laying down.

"Thank you." She said, turning the page to one of them nasty books she was always reading, not even taking the time to look at me. "You can put it on the nightstand and leave." She directed, pointing at the door like I was nothing but a stray dog.

"Queen come on. How long you gone be mad at me, baby?"

She didn't respond.

"Don't be like that, man. Don't you think you need to talk to me?" I asked, sitting on the bed while placing the tray over her lap as I rubbed up her legs.

"Want? want, want?" She repeated as she used her fork to stab a pancake, stuffing the food into her mouth. "It's all about what Serpent wants, right?" Zonnique sat up against the headboard with her arms crossed, talking to me like she wanted to kill me with the silverware. "And now that you messed up, you want to come talk to me? What do we need to talk about that we ain't talk about already? Huh, Serpent?" She rolled her eyes.

"Look I know I fucked up and I'm sorry, Nique, but I still want my family and most importantly, I still want us to get married. Just give me another chance to make it up to you." I pleaded.

She sucked her teeth in like she was listening to bullshit, taping her fingers with her arms still crossed; like I was wasting her valuable time.

"So, you expect me just to forgive you like that, huh?" She said snapping her fingers. "How can I trust you after you done cheated and got another woman pregnant? And how do I know you apologizing because you really mean it? You apologizing because you know that you got caught!"

"Come on, Nique. Do I really got to answer that?"

Her silence told me that I did.

"I'm apologizing because I know you didn't deserve that shit. Can you at least fuckin look at me? Nique, I'm still the same person that I was before." I told her, but she didn't say shit. "You talking to me as if you don't even know who I am anymore."

"Maybe I don't." She shrugged.

I dropped my head, grabbing her hand as I begged and plead. "Just give me a chance. What do I need to do to make it up to you? I'll do anything, just name it, Nique."

She exhaled and took a sip of the pulped orange juice,

thinking about my response. As she reached over to put the glass back on the nightstand, I could tell she didn't have no panties on under her T-shirt. I moved the breakfast tray out of the way, crawling up under her body to sit her pussy on my face.

"Really?" She asked trying to move back from me, but I locked her thighs in so that she couldn't move. "If you think some head bout to make everything better. You out of your, ohhhhhhhh," She dismissed her first thought, as my tongue opened up her chocolate folds, flicking hard on her clit. I knew she couldn't resist my tongue action.

"Oh, Serpent," Zonnique sounded like she had taken the load off, as I French kissed her clit.

I stuck my index finger in her hole. I had been trying to get her to squirt like the women in the porn flicks, but Zonnique hadn't learned that trick yet. As the tip of my tongue slithered into her slit, I could taste her creamy goodness on my lips. That pussy was tasting so good that I began talking to it, as if her pussy could hear me.

"I want you to still marry me, Nique." I blew my hot breath on her other eye, as I curved my index finger up her pussy and gave it a wiggle. Most females would have squirted by then, but not Zonnique.

"I don't know, Serpent…ohhhhhhh." Zonnique moaned, about to reach her climax.

"Don't tell me that you don't know." I said while forcing my tongue up her pussy hole. "I want you to Marry me, Nique." My nose went up and down her love box, as I sucked faster and faster, shaping my lips to match her black pussy perfectly.

"You, bout to make me…cum." She whined as I tasted her juices that spilled inside of my mouth.

I knew her clit was sensitive as I kissed it one more time before I got from under her ass. Zonnique just laid there. Hoping that I could win her over, I took out the ring and placed it back on her finger, waiting for her final response.

"I don't want us to cancel this wedding. Plus, I think I found the venue. You still have your wedding dress, and Zion still needs his family."

"I don't know about all of that right now, Serpent, but I'll think about it." She said getting up and heading over to the dresser to take out some clothes to put on for after her shower. When she walked into the bathroom, I took my clothes off and followed her ass in.

"This the type of nigga you is now? You leaving empty condom wrappers in your pants pocket's now?" I asked True as he came out of the bathroom, mushing him in the face before he pinned me up onto our bedroom door.

I had grown a suspicion because he had come in from work tired enough to fall asleep in his work clothes, snoring like he had just gotten some good pussy or something. I'd never seen True sleep in his clothes ever, nor has there ever been a day where he missed his alarm; not until the previous night.

When True overslept and I had to get up to cut off his alarm, that's what made me go through his pants pocket while he was in the shower.

"MERCEDEZ CALM YOUR ASS DOWN!" He roared, as I tried kicking him with my legs because they were the only things free.

"Why should I calm down, because you're a liar just like everybody else in my life? You're a liar True! You're a habitual liar True!"

"Don't compare me to everybody else in your life and stop calling me that!" He shouted. I like seeing True mad because that was the only time, I'd felt like he was still fighting for our relationship.

"Tell me True, who are you fuckin and do I know her?" I spat.

His strong grip still had me pinned to the wall. I knew True wasn't stupid enough to fuck someone I knew, but I wanted to know who he was willing to lose me over. I knew she was probably the opposite of me. True didn't have time to be fucking with immature prissy bitches like me, he was too mature and established for all of that. The only reason I thought he was still with me, was because we had such a long history.

If True was going to be messing around with someone else, it was going to be somebody he was feeling; a person who had ambitions and something going for herself. It would have made me feel a hell of a lot better if he'd done the same thing that I'd done to him, because maybe then I would have a good enough of an excuse to be fucking his step brother, but True shook his head in denial.

"You know I would never fuck with nobody you know. Especially not none of your bougie friends." He said, which I believed him. "If I let you go and tell you the truth, will you calm down and not get all crazy on me?" He asked, while looking into my eyes.

"I promise." I said with my fingers crossed, as he held my arms over my head.

"When, where and how?" I asked him as he let me go.

"I had sex with her yesterday, on the beach of a private Island. I gave her oral sex and we did it, missionary style." He admitted as his dick got a rise through his jeans.

I knew then he had to have really liked whoever the bitch was, to take her for a joyride in his helicopter. Then to take her to one of them private islands that he had never took me to. Oh, whoever the bitch was had to be real, special in his book. True never even let anybody touch his helicopter, let alone ride with him in it.

"How many times did you cheat on me, True?" I asked about to reach my boiling point, because he had really sat up there and told me the fuckin truth.

"Only once." He said.

BAM!

My reflexes reacted as I slapped True hard enough in the face, for the palm of my hand to sting. He grabbed the both of my wrist so hard that I thought with one twist, the bone was bound to break.

"Don't put your fuckin hands on me when I'm sitting up here telling your crazy ass the truth!" True barked, with fire in his eyes.

"I HATE YOU, TRUE! I OUGHTA FLUSH THIS RING DOWN THE TOILET AND CALL THE ENTIRE PROPOSAL OFF! I HATE YOU!" I threatened. All while trying to fight him, because it felt like what me and True had was just, falling apart.

"Call off the proposal then, Mercedez!" He said like he was testing me to do it. "I never even told you to go out and purchase the ring no way; knowing I never even proposed to you."

"So now you saying you don't want to be married to me?" I said crying with my ass on the floor, and my back against the door.

I knew he didn't propose to me, but I wanted to be married to him so bad that I was willing to buy a ring and force it on him. It wasn't like he ever disagreed with it. Hearing him say that he never even proposed to me hurt my feelings. Crocodile tears streamed down my face. True stood over me, bending down and taking a hold of my hand.

"I don't want you to feel like you gotta buy my love. These past few years, it's like we just steady growing apart. I love you and I know you love me, but is that enough for us to get married?" He asked me, heartfelt.

Is he really asking me this right now?

"True get the fuck off of me!" I said as I got up, going into the restroom while locking the door behind me.

It sounded like he was trying to break up with me and I wasn't going to let that happen. As I lifted the lid to the toilet seat, throwing up my insides, I flushed the toilet and stood up to try to get myself together. I stood back in the floor to ceiling mirror lifting the bottom of my shirt up, where a small pudge had formed. I knew time was running out and I needed to tell True soon.

"Mercedez," True said while knocking on the door. "The event for my father will be downstairs in a couple of hours."

"Go away, True! Just leave me alone," I cried.

I could hear True's footsteps travel down the stairs and out the front door. He wasn't the only one who had people to see and places to go. I changed into something simple, brushing my hair into a ponytail. Christmas was coming up and it was right around the time my cousin Bugatti had gotten taken to jail. Although I didn't look forward to visiting him, he probably missed me, and he was the only family member I needed to see for the holidays.

I called a private driver to come pick me up, going outside to see that True's Lamborghini was missing. I knew he had a charity event that day, because the private chef and other service people were downstairs, setting up for the event in the mansion. When the driver dropped me off at the federal prison, I wrote down Bugatti's offender information while waiting in the long line that wrapped outside and around the corner of the prison. In the line stood mostly women and children trying to see their loved ones behind the bars. I couldn't say that I was happy to see Bugatti, but I wasn't sad either. As I sat down at the silver, drilled in bench, focusing on Bugatti's face through the plex glass, I picked up the phone to listen to what he had to say.

"When the guards told me I had a visitor, the last person I thought that I would see was you. I always thought about how you were holding up in life until me and my cell mates seen you on television, twerking in one of them Sucker Free Sunday music videos that come on late at night." Bugatti said smiling a crooked smile, as he spoke through the bottom piece of the phone.

After all, of these years, you would think that he would be mad after not hearing from me. Then again, his business partner, Cyrus, had left him to rot in prison years ago. I was the one who made sure he had money on his books, enough for him to survive off, of every month. Bugatti was the splitting image of my uncle Sedan, with clay colored skin and green eyes like me; he didn't look like he aged in prison at all.

"You out of all people should know how I been holding up. Don't you remember selling me as a sex slave to Cyrus, right before you went to prison?" I asked, speaking back into the phone.

He looked to his left, then to his right. Scooting up with his elbows on the table, as he replied with his mouth touching the phone.

"When I got locked up, you were too young to understand that I didn't have that much of choice. I tried to take care of you the best way I could with what I had, but of course I didn't have much. When I was out on the streets hustling, it was tough having to take you with me in the blistering cold, seeing you sleep in the back seat of my car; I knew that wasn't the life for you. But I was the only blood member you had left, so what was a nigga to do? I couldn't just let you get lost in the system. You had already suffered so much when your parents died; I only did what I had to do at the time. And if you feel like I betrayed you, then I'm sorry you feel that way, Pretty Red."

"Don't you dare call me Pretty Red!" I said pointing my finger and touching the plex glass. "My father is the only one who could ever call me that. Don't you ever call me by that name again. You hear me?"

"Hey, you got it. Heard you loud and clear, boss lady." Bugatti said with his hands raised up as if he surrendered. "You know how word spreads fast around the streets, it just come a lil slower when you in jail." He said with a slurred accent. "I guess from being locked up for so long." I listened as he continued with the conversation.

"I heard about what happened to Cyrus. I'm glad somebody decided to put his lights out before I did."

I was silent because I felt the same way. Only three people knew about me being sold to the Blackwell's, and one of them were now dust.

"I'm glad you came down here to see me. It's something I think you need to know." Bugatti said. The way his lips moved slow, as if he was trying to choose his words carefully, had told me that the news he was getting ready to tell me was important.

"What do you mean, it's something you think I need to know? What else do I need to know that I don't know already?" I asked in a questioning tone.

"I'm not really your big cousin, and your mother isn't my auntie Scarlett, either."

"Then who are you to me and my mother?"

He licked his lips and said, "Scarlett and my father Sedan was having a love affair; it started way before the both of us was even born. From what Sedan told me before he passed, everybody knew about the affair, even your father, but I don't think he wanted to believe it."

"And what makes you think that?" I said. He was starting to annoy me, sounding like a know it all.

"Because your aunt Scarlett is my mother, which makes

you my sister."

My tongue had felt dry. My mother would never betray my father like that.

"I don't believe it, Bugatti." I said, closing my eyes to stop the warm tears that were behind my eyelids. "Why should I believe anything you say?"

"Because I got the proof right here." He said taking out an old folded up piece of paper from out of his shirt, holding it up to the plex glass with a smile. "You see Mercedez, you don't have to call me your cousin Bugatti anymore, you can call me your big brother now."

As I read the names with the two signatures on the birth certificate, I couldn't do nothing but get up and drop the phone. Everything in my life had been a lie. I was just like my mother, a certified whore.

"This the place I was telling you that I wanted our wedding to be at, I just have to pull a couple of strings first." Serpent told me as we walked inside of this grand ball room, dressed in red carpet attire.

Tables were draped down in crystal tablecloths and, chairs were covered in cream with giant gold bows on the back. Lights cascaded above the ceiling and people filled the tables.

"I love it!" I shouted. "This is where I want our wedding at; I don't want to look nowhere else."

Serpent and I were at this charity event, where we were donating a toy in memory of his late stepfather. The event was held in this gray stone mega mansion, reminding me of one of them modern castles from the middle ages. Since Serpent and I had called the wedding back on, he wanted me to join him for the evening.

"I want you to meet my stepbrother, and his fiancé." Serpent said with his hand on my lower back, guiding me through a small crowd of people on the floor.

"You never told me you had a stepbrother." I said, wondering why after all, of these years, he didn't mention him before.

Serpent walked in front of me and tapped the shoulder of a guy, who was having a conversation with the Mayor. When the guy turned around, I almost fainted on the dance floor.

"Zonnique I want you to meet my stepbrother, True Blackwell." He introduced, shaking hands with True, who didn't take his eyes off, of me.

"True, I want you to meet my fiancé, Zonnique Jones. Will yours not be accompanying us this evening?"

"She's having a hard time with everything." He told Serpent before his eyes zoomed on me. "Nice to meet you, Zonnique." True reached for my hand as his lips brushed the middle of my forehand. I took my hand away and placed it to my side; True was bold as fuck.

"Nique, bae, are you okay? Do you need to take a seat?" Serpent asked, noticing my awkward stance.

"I just think I need to get something to drink." I told him, relieved that he walked me over to the bar. I'd had sex with Serpent's stepbrother and didn't even much know it.

"I see a lot of people here from the job, I'ma go around and speak." Serpent told me. "Be right back, baby."

You would think as his fiancé he would want to introduce me, but nope. Leave it to Serpent, to do his own thing. When he left me standing at the bar, I eased into a seat, paying for a small bottle of water.

"You look too beautiful to be sitting at a bar alone." True complimented as he came over and stood next to me.

I wanted to be mad at him, but why did he have to always smell so good?

"Let me have two vodkas on the rocks," He told the bar tender as he waited for him to fix his drinks.

"Why didn't you just be true to me? Why not just tell me that you knew?" I asked as I took a sip of my water, twisting the cap back onto the bottle to sit on the bar.

"I didn't find out till later on and by that time, I had already developed feelings for you."

"Yeah right," I said, dismissing his comment. "We had a one-night, stand and that was it."

"If that's what you wanna call it, but I know you felt the connection." He said as his bare hand slid under the bar's table, giving my thigh a squeeze, before he found his way into the seat of my panties.

His thick fingers fondled with my pussy lips, as goosebumps formed between my thighs. My pussy pulsed like a heartbeat, bringing me back to that time True gave me my first real orgasm. As I gently moved his hand from my thigh, True licked his middle finger like he wanted another taste of me.

"I'm getting married, True. And from what Serpent tells me, so are you." I reminded him, by showing him the ring on my finger.

"I never even proposed to her, Zonnique. Do you see a ring on my finger?"

"Sounds like a personal issue, if you ask me." I said as the bar tender placed two drinks in front of True, who took out this gold money clip, tipping the bartender too high of a tip. I turned my head, gazing across the room. Serpent was sitting in between two beautiful women, laughing and carrying on like he was a single man. Ugh, I swear he was getting on my everlasting nerves.

"Remind me why he left you sitting here?" True asked as he gave me a drink, before taking a swig of his own.

"He's just talking to his employees; No Biggie." I shrugged.

"Them two women aren't employees. They're friends of my fiancé."

I twisted my neck around to see Serpent getting up, walking outside with the two women. I dropped my shoulders and finished drinking on my glass of vodka.

Guess I know where Serpent and I stand....

I didn't have time to look hurt in front of True, or anybody as a matter of fact.

"Where's the bathroom?" I asked. Guess True could see the *I didn't give a fuck* expression on my face.

"Come on, I'll show you." He said.

True helped me up out of my seat as he led the way, holding my hand like I was his woman. I couldn't even lie to myself, the feeling to be his, even just for one night, felt good. I followed him out into the lobby, walking into the nice restroom, bracing my hands around the gold ceramic sink. I didn't even know why I was even trying with the nigga and I couldn't help that True was doing something to me. I looked into the mirror trying to fix myself. Going into my clutch, taking out my lippie to re-gloss my lips, I heard someone come into the restroom.

"What are you doing in here True?"

He didn't say anything as he stepped up to me, tucking a side of my hair behind my ear. Our lips slowly crashed as we sped up kissing with our tongues. True picked me up and sat me on the restroom's counter, jerking my dress up my thighs.

"True, stop." His teeth found my nude panties. He slid them slowly off my legs, enough for goose bumps to come across my body.

"Why should I?" He asked before his hand reached over my thigh as he opened me up.

"Because you're my fiancé's stepbrother. What if somebody comes in?" I asked.

"We'll tell em no one is here then." He whispered while his finger hit the lights.

It was pitch black, but his touch was making my pussy

wet. His long, muscled tongue found my clit, sending vibrations through my body. All I could do was tilt my head back onto the mirror.

"True I'm going to squirt if you don't stop! ohhhh don't stop," I whispered, feeling True twirl his tongue on my spot, before he stuck his tongue into my hole.

"Can you squirt for me, Nique? I want you to squirt for True. Squirt." He demanded while he still had a hold on my pussy.

That alone was turning me on, as he began making this buzzing sound with his lips, paying extra attention to my clit. I couldn't hold my orgasm. The sound of my juices, were like running water that spilled onto the floor.

"True, I'm squirting." I cried.

An intense feeling began to take over my body. If it wasn't for me having on a black dress, I wouldn't have been able to hide my secretions that seeped through the material.

"I wanna talk to you about something." He said as I got up off the counter.

We walked out of the restroom, down the hall and on top of the ledge of the balcony. The view was dark, but you could still see the wind move the leaves in the sculptured trees. I wouldn't have been so willing to go with True if Serpent wouldn't have left me to talk to two bimbos, at an event that he wanted me to accompany him to. True leaned his hands over the ledge.

"My father married Serpent's mother when we were just teenagers. Serpent and his mother were living with us for only a short amount of time, before my father and his mother separated." True told me.

"So, your father and Mama Joyce never divorced?" I asked.

"Naw." True said. "From what I know they never did. I didn't even know that Serpent and I were working at the same place until my father passed and he took over the family's company."

As I listened to True, I couldn't help but respect the fact that he was being so honest with me. He didn't even owe me an explanation, yet he told me anyway. I knew all, of it was wrong, catching feelings for True, but damn it felt so good!

"Why are you telling me this?" I asked him.

True grabbed my face. "I just wanted to keep it a thousand with you."

He grabbed me by the side of my neck, pulling me into him. I closed my eyes and our tongues became tongue tied. I didn't open my eyes, until I start feeling like someone was staring at me.

"What the fuck! Is this the bitch you been fucking?" A woman with an empty bottle of liquor charged at True, coming from behind the glass doors that lead to the balcony. The ring she was waving on her finger, had told me that she was True's fiancé.

"Is you drunk right now, Mercedez?" True said as he held her down, to stop her from fighting him.

The name sounded familiar; I squinted my eyes at her. She most definitely looked like the women from the ultrasound appointment; the same woman that claimed she was pregnant by Serpent. If I wasn't a classy woman who didn't believe in girl code, I would've told True about her trifling ass. But to prevent me from going to jail and placing hands on a pregnant woman, I picked up the bottom of my dress.

"Zonnique wait," I ignored True, heading back downstairs into the ballroom to search for Serpent. I was ready for him to take me home.

"There you are, baby. I came back in bout a minute ago; where were you?" Serpent asked causing attention from the guest at the event, as he grabbed a handful of my ass, with the smell of liquor on his breathe.

"Let's fuck on the dance floor." Serpent was half drunk and obnoxious.

"Serpent, stop."

He shoved his tongue into my mouth, forcing his rough hand up my dress. I swiped his hand away. Serpent became still in place, as he rubbed his fingers together, like they were sticky. He smelled his hand then gave me a look of disgust.

"What the fuck, Nique! Where the fuck are your panties?" He asked while burning his eyes at me suspiciously. True had never gave me back my panties when he took them off, of me.

"Let's go to the car now, Nique!" Serpent shouted as he yanked me by my hair while dragging me out of the mansion.

The skin on my back burned from being scraped across the pavement. Patches of my follicles was being ripped out of my scalp, as Serpent shoved me into the vehicle.

"What are you doing, Serpent? What's wrong?" I asked as tears ran down my face, running my fingers through my scalp, collecting balls of my own loose hair.

"You fucking that nigga? Is you fucking my stepbrother, True?" Serpent's eyes had turned to slits. "What you think this a game or something?" He asked as he started the car, knocking down the French gates to the mansion, all while speeding wildly down the road. As we made it onto the freeway, all I could think about was True.

"I should be asking you the same thing. Being that you're the one who got True's fiancé pregnant!"

BAM!

My head twisted back as I spat out a glob of sour blood into my hands, in disbelief that Serpent had just hit me.

"Yeah, I got his bitch pregnant, but at least I'm man enough to admit it. Now did you fuck True or do I have to ask you the question one more time!" Serpent shouted, driving erratically, while switching lanes.

"We didn't have sex, Serpent." My voice said barely over a whisper, too scared that I would agitate him again. "What are you doing Serpent? Why are we pulling over?" I asked him.

He veered the car onto the side of the freeway. His silence scared me as he placed the gear into park, reaching over my side to push my seat back.

"You want to get me back, by having a baby with my brother, True? Is that why you fucked him? Answer me!"

BAM!

"Serpent, stop! Please! You're hurting me!" I cried.

"Fuck That!" He spat, as he used his knuckles to hit me like a full grown man.

My body felt like I had been bitten by a million of fire ants. Every bone in my body felt broken as he used my body like his personal punching bag, breathing like a crazed maniac.

"I love you, Zonnique. Can't you see that?"

When he stopped with his blows, he kissed me on my split lip, before driving back down the freeway.

When I swerved into our apartments, I picked Zonnique up and threw her body over my shoulders; being that she didn't have the strength to walk on her own two feet. I was outside of the mansion talking to Mercedez's friends trying to see if she was going to have the abortion or not, when I overheard Mercedez screaming at True over the balcony. I didn't think anything of it, not until I saw Zonnique walking back into the ball room. Then when I smelled the sex on my fingers, I knew Mercedez was talking about her. I had never put my hands on a woman before, but Zonnique needed to learn her lesson. Maybe then she would never try to fuck over me again.

I entered the house, carrying her marked up body up the stairs; taking her dress off by unzipping the back. She winced as I got a closer look at the purple blotches of bruises and fresh cuts on her back. I placed her into the shower, turning on the warm water as I took a seat on the toilet. Zonnique laid in a fetal position while crying on the shower floor.

"You beat me! You really just beat me, Serpent. Why would you do this to me?"

"I'm sorry that I had to beat you, but you made me do it, man. If you wouldn't have been fucking True, none of this would have ever happened."

Zonnique said nothing. All I could hear was her whimpering. I grabbed a washcloth and soap, lathering up the suds, before washing her battered and bruised body. As her blood washed down the drain, I scooped her naked body into my arms, placing her into our bed.

"Where's my phone?" She asked as she began trying to feel for it in the bed.

I wasn't about to let her call the laws on me or anybody else for that matter. So, I'd stomped on it with my boots.

"Your phone is no longer in service." I told her, sprinkling the broken bits of her cell in front of her face. She deeply sighed before turning over on her side to cry some more.

"And don't think you're going to work tomorrow, I had already texted your boss and told him that you'd be out sick, till further notice."

"Why are you doing this?" She asked, tears falling onto her pillow.

"Because I love you and if I can't have you, no one else can. If you think you're going to play me by running off into the sunset with True, I'm here to tell you that he will never leave you for his fiancé. You probably were just something for him to fuck. Besides, I will never let you be with someone else and that's on my son, Zion Mckinney."

As Zonnique pulled the covers over her head, I closed the door; locking it from the inside out. I was going to do whatever I had to do to keep her away from True. Even if that meant locking her up in our bedroom and throwing away the key.

"SERPENT!" My Mama Joyce called me from down the stairs.

Fuck! I'd forgotten to lock the door when I carried Zonnique up the stairs.

"The door was unlocked so I let myself in." She called out as she made her way up the stairs, limping with her cane while Zion ran from behind her.

"Hey daddy!" He shouted as he came up and hugged me. "Where's mommy?" His innocent face asked.

"Yeah where is Zonnique? Mama Joyce asked as she made it up to the top of the staircase. "I've been calling her phone to tell her that Zion and I were on our way and she hasn't been answering. Is her phone dead?"

"She ended up breaking her phone when we got back into the house." I said, trying to keep my eyes away from her as I gave Zion a hug.

"What's wrong with your hands? Why do you have blood on your knuckles, son?" When I hesitated to answer, Mama Joyce went straight towards our bedroom, pulling on the doorknob to see that it was locked.

"Zonnique!" She yelled, banging her open hand on the front of the door. "Are you in there, baby?! If so, say something!"

When she didn't hear an answer, Mama Joyce didn't waist anytime to kick the door down with her cane. I was astonished at her strength because for someone who had suffered a stroke, she was able to get the door open with one try.

"Mommy!" Zion said as he ran over to Zonnique's side of the bed, taking the cover off, of her body. "What's wrong with my mommy!" Zion shouted, sobbing as he stared at Zonnique's body.

"Oh my god!" Mama Joyce said as she clutched the pearls around her neck. "Serpent what did you do to her?!"

"Please, Mama Joyce, just get my son out of here. I don't want him to see me like this." Zonnique cried, reaching for Mama Joyce's hand; not even having enough energy to lift her head.

"Zion baby, go downstairs into the car, lock the door while you wait on granny Joyce. Okay?" Mama Joyce asked sweetly.

When Zion ran downstairs with a face full of tears, Mama Joyce waited to hear Zion close the front of the door before lifting her cane as she came towards me, clucking me upside my head until I fell onto my knees.

"ARE YOU OUT OF YOUR MIND?! YOU WANT YOUR SON TO BE A WOMAN BEATER? I DIDN'T RAISE YOU TO PUT YOUR HANDS ON A WOMAN! YOUR REAL DAD MIGHT NOT HAVE BEEN PRESENT IN YOUR LIFE, BUT THAT DON'T GIVE YOU A RIGHT TO LAY YOUR HANDS ON A WOMAN YOU CLAIM TO LOVE!" She shouted, drawing back again with her wooden cane. "You wanna be mad at somebody? Be mad at me!"

"Damn Mama! Zonnique was having sex with True! Alright." I told her, backing up from her as I tried blocking her licks. "Ahhhhhhh!" I screamed while tumbling down the flight of stairs, causing my head to hit the wall as I landed on the bottom of my ass.

Mama Joyce limped down the staircase slowly, lifting my chin up with her cane. "I wouldn't give a damn if she was fuckin God Almighty himself. You don't ever put your hands on a woman, ever! Ya hear me talking to you boy?"

"What do I need to do to fix it, mama? Tell me," I pressed, bringing my hands up to my face as I cried. I didn't know if Zonnique would ever forgive me.

"Your best bet is to go somewhere else for tonight. Maybe check into a hotel room until things cool off with you and Zonnique." Mama Joyce suggested, trying to console me.

"But what about me and Zonnique? I still want things to work out between us."

"Well, then you better hope the mother of your child is still here when you come back. I wouldn't blame her if she isn't. You're my son and I want the best for you, but you got to want it for yourself."

After Mama Joyce left with Zion, I knew it was no coming back from what I'd done. I dreadfully got into my car. Pulling my gun out from up under the seat, I logged into Facebook, and went on live with the gun pressed against my temple.

"You see what Zonnique made me do?" I asked the people on my live video, introducing them to my pistol named Montana.

"I oughta fuckin kill her for fucking my stepbrother." I said as I searched for True's business page. Since I had him as a friend on facebook, I tagged him in the video, directing the message to him personally.

"True Blackwell, you think you better than me, bro? You think you better because you Cyrus's son?" I asked pointing the gun at the phone's camera while talking. "Can't be too much better than me. That's why I got your fiancé pregnant! Yeah, I bet she didn't tell you all of that. Ask her how I ate her pussy out in the bed that she shares with you! Yeah, the jokes on you motherfucker!" I laughed out loud, while waving the gun into the air. "Mercedez's such a damn hoe; the only reason she trying to keep that baby is cause I took over your daddy's company! Ya'll wanna know how I moved my way up the company? I made Cyrus sign the company over to me, right before I killed him! The filthy dirty rich bastard deserved it!"

I started reading one of the comments that scrolled up on the screen of my live video from Zonnique's friend, Myrah.

I was on board with you and Zonnique getting married because I wanted Zion to see that his mother and father could be a family, but now that you' showing your true colors, I hope Zonnique leaves your trifling ass. That's why you deserve everything you going through right now. You can't do evil for evil and expect good to be done to you. I'm on my way to the house to check on my friend, and if you're still there by the time I get there, I will call the laws and watch them take your ass to jail. Play with me if you want to.

"Aye Myrah, shut the fuck up and go find you a man!" I told her before exiting out of the live video.

I knew she meant what she said, so I started the car and proceeded to drive out of the apartment complex. By the time I got back, Zonnique better had come to her senses.

When I parked into the parking lot of the motel, I didn't have enough money to check into a room, so I went down to the bar, buying a fifty-cent watered down alcoholic drink, with the last hundred-dollar bill in my pocket. I sat off into the corner of the room, as I began playing the slot machine. I was addicted to possibly making a hit. I had been swimming in loans and had already ran through my savings. Zonnique didn't even know that I'd spent all, of the money that was supposed to go towards her dream wedding. I didn't even tell her how I had been blowing through the company's money, and I needed to dig myself out of a hole.

I was going to sit at that slot machine all day and night, if it killed me. All I needed was one lucky shot to hit the jack pot.

I kept having the same reoccurring dream. Where I was standing in the middle of an open grassy field, running towards the both of my parents. I could hear my father calling my name in the distance, right on the other side of the hill. I was so close, only a hand reach away from meeting his fingertips. Just when I was about to touch him, the both of my parents evaporated before I woke.

I tried to dry my tear stained face. True's missing pillow on his side of the bed, told me that he was sleeping in another part of the house. He'd always said once we'd start to fall asleep mad at each other, he would no longer be happy. I had a feeling that he had been feeling unhappy for a while.

My phone began to ring from the inside of my clutch, that found its way under the bed. Still Woozy and half asleep, I got out of the bed crawling onto all fours. The only person that was important enough for me to get out of bed and answer the phone for, was Diamond or Princess.

"Hello," I answered with a low slurred voice, as I sat on the gold floor.

"Girl I'm glad you picked up the phone. I need to tell you what Serpent did before it gets back to True."

"What? What did Serpent do?" I asked, now fully awake.

"Don't tell me you don't remember what happened last night?" Diamond asked.

The hammering headache from the lingering hang-over, told me that I did. Basing on the dress I was still in, after I'd gotten white girl wasted at the charity event, True must've placed me into bed.

"After you fought True, Serpent and his fiancé, the one who was standing on the balcony with True, had got into it. Serpent dragged her up out of the mansion. Princess said she saw the whole thing."

"That's what her ass gets, but what does that have to do with me and True." I inquired.

"Serpent went online and aired out ya'lls business. He even had enough balls to tag True."

As my heart felt like it was about to thump out of my chest, I tried catching my breathe as Diamond said, "I sent you the video. Everybody on the internet is calling you a whore; and get this, people are making memes about you with the hash tag, *a stepbrother's whore.* You're even receiving hate mail."

I tuned Diamond out as I opened up the video clip that she'd sent me. My stomach churned as Serpent exposed something I'd been trying to hide from True for so long.

"There goes my reputation." I said. I could kiss my modeling career goodbye.

"Forget about your reputation, what about your relationship with True?"

I walked into the master bathroom, going into the medicine cabinet for a bottle of sleeping pills; I didn't want to feel anything anymore. I didn't want to live anymore; I was ready to join my mother and father.

"Hello, Mercedez are you there?!"

With Diamond on speaker phone, I slid my back against

the wall. I said a prayer, ready to meet my maker. I unscrewed the child safety top, emptying the entire bottle of pills into my mouth and swallowed.

"Mercedez Taylor, I know you hear me talking to you! What are you going to do about True?" Diamond's voice started to sound from afar.

As I laid onto the tiled gold floor my body began to feel numb.

I got up from the couch inside of my home office; I thought I'd heard Mercedez walking in the hallway. As I walked up the banister of stairs, the light glowed from under the bathroom. I wanted to check on her, so I knocked on the door waiting for her to answer. I didn't hear her using the toilet, nor did I hear the shower running, so I knocked on the door again.

"Mercedez," I said. "we need to talk." It sounded like someone was trying to talk to her on the phone. As I twisted the doorknob opening the door, my eyes gloated at Mercedez, whose body was laid out on the floor.

"Cedez?!" I gasped. "What did you fuckin take?!"

I snatched the pill bottle that was in the palm of her hand. The label read Ambien. As I maneuvered my hands under Mercedez's body, I brought her towards the toilet. I raised the seat and stuck my two fingers towards the back of her throat. The sound of liquid from the contents of pills, splashed into the toilet. Her eyes were chink; her head slumped over the seat.

"I need you to keep your eyes open, Cedez! Don't die on me like this!"

She felt cold as clams as I lightly slapped the side of her rosy cheeks, trying to make sure she stayed alert. I pulled her into the jacuzzi, hoping the cold water would help.

"Uhhhhhhhh, uhhhhhhhh." The way Mercedez moaned while barely keeping her eyes open, told me still had a chance to live.

With Mercedez in my arms, I grabbed my keys and raced out of the house. I carried her to the car, buckling her dangling body in the passenger seat; speeding through traffic as fast I can to the hospital. When I made it to the urgent care, I sat in the waiting room, finally having a chance to get on my phone, waiting for time to pass.

As I stumble across the video of Serpent on Facebook, I paced the floor of the empty lobby, clenching the phone into my hand. Serpent had confessed to being, the one behind my father's death and I wanted revenge. Yeah, I was upset at Mercedez for doing what she did but that didn't mean she deserved to pay for it with her life. Granted, I could no longer be with her, me and Serpent would always be blood and he was going to have to see me; especially if he harmed even a hair on Zonnique's head. I wished I could've call her but we had never exchanged numbers. One thing she did tell me, was her full name.

I scrolled to the top of the page on Facebook, typing her first and last name into the search. Only one profile had come up, but I knew it was her. I could recognize her beautiful smile and eyes from anywhere. I tapped on the profile relieved that it wasn't private. She didn't have a lot of photos. I was looking at a picture of her in front of a high school, dressed in her cap and gown with glasses on her face. She had to have been standing in between her mother and father, who both had doctor coats on.

I tapped out of the photo and noticed that she had only one recent picture. It had to be a picture that she'd taken with one of her friends. They were standing in front of a bunch of mirrors, and her friend was hugging her. Zonnique was smiling in a wedding dress. I knew then that they must've gotten married. I know that, that alone should've made me change my feelings about her, but it didn't. I wanted to see her. I needed to see her. I wanted to make sure she was okay.

I decided to click on the friend that tagged her in the

picture. I wasn't the type of guy to slide through a woman's DM. That was childish to me, but this was under different circumstances. I inboxed her friend Myrah, asking about the whereabouts of Zonnique. I didn't know if her friend would respond to me or not, but I had to at least try.

I walked over to the service table, fixing a small cup of coffee. Through all of this, I just wanted Mercedez to pull through.

"True Blackwell," The doctor called out to me. "My name is Doctor Jones."

I squinted because he looked familiar to me.

"How is she doing?" I asked. "Is she going to make it?"

"Unfortunately, she ended up losing the baby. The toxicology report showed that Mercedez took over a well, number of pills that could have killed a horse. If it wasn't for you bringing her in right when you did, things would have been fatal. She's lucky to even be alive. She had her stomach pumped and is waking up now from being heavily sedated. She's probably feeling groggy, but you can see her now."

I thanked the doctor before catching the elevator to Mercedez's room.

When I walked into the room, Mercedez was dressed in a hospital gown, sitting up in the bed. I sat across from her at the foot of the bed but before I could say anything to her, she looked at me and said, "I'm so sorry. I didn't know how to tell you, that I was cheating on you with Serpent. I know you must hate me now; join the rest of the world."

"I could never hate you, I love you. And even though we're breaking up, I don't want you to ever feel like you have to kill yourself." I said, taking out a pamphlet with a plane ticket to China inside.

"What's this?" Mercedez asked as she looked through the pamphlet, before picking up the oneway plane ticket.

"I was going to surprise you with it the night of the charity event, but I never got a chance to. I booked a one-year retreat for you in China. You always talked about how you wanted to start over fresh; I hope that maybe this can help you. I want you to spend however much time you need to get yourself together."

"How can I ever repay you?" Mercedez asked, glancing at me in confusion.

"Don't worry about it." I told her as a nurse walked Princess and Diamond into the room; they both had gift bags, and some get well balloons.

"Take care of yourself," I told Mercedez before giving her a hug and a kiss on the cheek, going into Doctor Jones office next.

"If I told you that I knew your daughter, Zonnique Jones, would you be willing to see her and meet your five-year old grandson?" I asked him as he looked up at me from his desk, while sitting in his chair.

"And what do you know about my only daughter?" He asked.

"I know that your daughter is intelligent and works as an ultrasound technician. I know that she can be a book worm and when she's not reading, she's being a mother to her son. I know she misses you a lot and would want you to meet Zion. But most importantly, I know I'm in love with your daughter."

Doctor Jones got up slowly, shaking my hand as he said, "All I wanted, was for a man to see what I've always saw in her. I never thought Serpent was the one for her. I was too hard on her as a father, I've kept that guilt with me for years. I know her mother and I miss her dearly. True, can you bring me my daughter and only grandson?"

"I will, but first I have to find her."

"You and Zion could spend Christmas Eve with me, really it's fine; however much time you need." Myrah said as she tried to make the downstairs bedroom to her three-bedroom town home, comfortable enough for me and Zion to sleep in.

She dressed the Queen, wooden sleigh bed with a fitted white sheet and white patterned comforter, pulling a corner of the comforter back for me to get in the bed.

"Thank you again for having my back, Myrah," I told her as I sat on the bed, opening the traveling suitcase that was packed with a few of me and Zion's clothes.

"What are we going to do about Christmas?" Zion asked as he held on to my hand, standing up by the bed. I tried to force a smile, by putting on a happy face.

"As long as I have you, I'm always going to be okay." I kissed Zion on the cheek, and he gave me a smile back.

"Why don't I show you to the pantry? I have a jar full of chocolate chip cookies." Myrah said to Zion, as they walked out of the room and to the kitchen.

I was sad for the broken relationship between Serpent and, I. I wanted my happily ever after but after Myrah showed me Serpent's video, on top of seeing Zion's face when Serpent beat me up, I never wanted Zion to witness me go through that again.

Myrah was nice enough to light a few scented candles around the guest bathroom; she even made me one of them spiritual baths, filling the bath with the petals that she prayed over. As my bubble bath water ran, I went through my suitcase, taking out a change of clothes. I waited for the water to get warm, before stripping out of my dirty clothes and getting into the tub of water. It stung a bit, from some of the bruises that was slowing trying to heal, but the stings settled and began to feel soothing towards my skin. I sat back and tried to relax. The smooth, sound of *Tru* by Lloyd, played on the counter from the blue tooth speaker. The song couldn't have come on at a better time because I instantly thought about True. I wished he was there, just waiting for me on the bed. I wished he could kiss me on every part of my scarred body and tell me that everything would be okay. But the way he held down, his fiancé, I knew he was willing to fight for her. I wanted Serpent to fight for me, but I had no more fight left for him. Zion and I would be spending the holidays with just us.

I got out of the tub, letting my hair fall down my back as I added some lotion to my skin. I decide to let my skin air dry as I blew the candles out, before walking back into the bedroom.

"Is it True, did you marry him?"

"True?" I said shocked to see him. "Serpent and I didn't get married. What are you doing here?" I asked, wishing I would have grabbed the towel to cover myself.

"Myrah told me you were here. I wanted to make sure you and Zion were okay."

"We're fine." I said. "What about you and your fiancé?"

"I saw the video. We're no longer together, but she's okay. She's on a plane to live in China." He informed.

"Good for her." I mumbled. "If you will excuse me for a second. I need you to step outside while I change."

"Not until I ask you something." He said. Curious, I stood there, naked as day.

"When I think about you, I know that no one else will ever hold my heart the way you do, and I want a place in you and Zion's world. With that being said, Zonnique Jones, will you marry me?"

"Come on, True, you don't really mean that." I said while turning my back and folding my arms.

"No, but I do. My love for you is true." The way we gazed into each other's eyes, told me he meant everything he'd said.

"I don't want you to hide your body from me. I love everything about it. From your stretch marks, all the way to your love handles." True said as he kissed a bruise that Serpent left on my shoulder. Those words made cum drip from my pussy. As I fell onto the bed, True climbed on top of me. I could get used to being in that position. He wouldn't keep his eyes off, of me; opening my pink slit as he guided his erect muscle into my middle.

"I'm falling in love with you, True." I said as he gracefully pushed in and out of me; my juices lubricated his penis.

"I love you too, Zonnique. I love your black, creamy pussy." True sung as his dick woke up my every sense. His long stick glided around my pussy, causing me to moan as I scratched into his back.

"Don't you ever try to hide your body from me again. Look at me before I cum." He directed as he dug into me even deeper.

"I won't do it ever again, True! I love your dick, True! My pussy's cumming!"

As I came onto his dick, we laid there until one of us decided to speak again.

"I want you and Zion to come with me." True said as I changed into my clothes.

∞ ∞ ∞

"Where are you taking us?" I asked him as the three of us flew inside of his helicopter.

"There's somebody who's been wanting to see you." He said.

When we landed, True was covering my eye's, before I could even get out of the helicopter.

"Where are you taking us, True?"

It felt like I was walking forever, until he took the blind fold off, of me. I scanned around the four white walls filled with plaques, to see that I was standing in my father's doctor's office.

"Zonnique?" I turned around to see my mother frantically running into the office, as she wrapped her arms around me. I couldn't help but burst out into tears, grateful that True had cared about me enough to bring me to my parents.

"It's really my baby! It's really my baby." My mother sobbed while rocking me back and forth.

"And who is this little guy?" She asked as Zion popped up from behind the chair.

"Hi! My name is Zion, what's yours?"

"Zion, I'm your grandmother. Come over here and let me pinch those cheeks. He is just precious!" She said as she admired him, still crying.

"Father?" I said, getting out of my chair to run to him. He didn't say anything, probably from shock as he hugged me slowly.

"I'm so proud of you, and I love you, daughter. I'm sorry if I didn't tell you enough." My father said as tears came down from his eyes.

"I forgive you father and I love you too."

Zion ran to my father and he picked him up; playing with him as he tossed him up and down into the air. I walked over to True, who was sitting in the lobby. As we gave each other a kiss on the lips, he seemed occupied with something else.

"What's wrong, baby?" I asked him. His eyes focused on the news on the flat screen that hung above the wall of the lobby.

"My father's company is going out of business."

Serpent

"Sir you've been here gambling for twenty-four hours straight and the bar is now closed. Do you have someone I can call to come give you a ride home? Maybe an Uber or a Lyft?" The female bar tender from the motel asked, clearly looking like she was ready to clock out and be done with her shift.

With heavy bags under my eyes and a night of restless sleep, I wiped the dribble of drool from the side of my face. Waking up in front of the slot machine had become my new high. I sized the woman up and down, she wasn't as pretty as Mercedez or Zonnique, but she could get a pass since I was desperate.

"Naw, I don't have anyone to pick me up but maybe you could take me home with you." I flirted with her, but she only gave me this displeasing look.

She walked away as I blew my breathe into the cup of my hand, nearly burning my nose hairs from the smell. I reeked of alcohol, mixed with a combination of shit. I ran my tongue across my teeth, tasting the thick buildup of plaque. My tongue had felt like a thick sheet of sandpaper. I knew I was a complete mess, but I was thinking about Zonnique. I took out my cell dialing her number, hanging right back up because I remembered that I'd broke the phone.

I walked outside into the parking lot searching for my car, trying to figure out why it was even missing. Then I remembered that I hadn't paid the car note in about six months, and the bank had probably repossessed it. With no wheels and a dead cellphone, I walked across the street to the gas station.

Standing in front of a payphone, I patted myself down. Pulling the inside of each pocket out, I realized that I didn't even have a dollar to my name. I made my way to the nearest bus stop. As I sat on the bench, looking raggedy enough to be mistaken for homeless, I thanked the Metro bus driver, who was friendly enough to allow me to get on the bus for free.

When the bus dropped me off in front of my apartments, I tore off the orange eviction notice that was taped on the front door, expecting for Zonnique to still be in the bed.

"Zonnique are you home!" I called out as I climbed up the stairs, hoping she was willing to reconciliate. When I didn't see her laying in the bed, I searched around our two-bedroom apartment.

"Hunni where are you?!" I went looking for Zonnique in our son's bedroom.

I thought that maybe she was reading a book to Zion, but when I didn't see him in the room either, a gut feeling was telling me that she'd left. I went back into our bedroom and spotted the diamond ring, that I'd gifted to her on the night stand. Still not wanting to believe that she had left me for good, I opened our small walk in closet to see that all her clothes and shoes on her side of the shelf, were missing. She only left a few framed pictures on the top shelf. The same family pictures that we had taken around the holidays the previous year. I'd let a couple of coins air my head up, when all Zonnique wanted was for us to get married and be a family.

I walked out of the house and around the corner, going to the only person that would accept me. I unlocked the door to my Mama Joyce's house, going straight into my bedroom. All my snakes were slithering in their enclosures. I lifted the lid of one of the enclosures, taking one of my vipers by the head. I wanted to know what real pain felt like. I opened the snake's mouth, to see it withdraw four sharp poisonous fangs, I held out my wrist, ready to feel the pain.

"Serpent, son, what are you doing?" Mama Joyce asked, with the look of startle in her eye.

"I lost everything mama; the company is going down the drain, my money is a bust. Most importantly, Zonnique and Zion had left me, and I know my family will never come back." I cried with the snake an inch away from my wrist.

Mama Joyce slowly came towards me as if she was trying to talk me out of pulling a trigger.

"The snake, as a symbol of Satan, has wound its way around the human heart and filled us with its poison. Try as we might, we cannot rid ourselves of its influence." My mother quoted from the bible as she grabbed the venomous snake by the head, allowing the snake to slither back into its tank, before grabbing me.

As I cried in her arms on the floor of my bedroom, it all made sense to what she was telling me. I was born with something I couldn't rid myself of. *Poison.*

"Promise me if he's in there, you won't kill him? Zonnique asked, as we got to the oil and energy facility.

"I promise I won't, for you and Zion's sake. But now that the business is closing, I don't know what I'm going to do about a job."

"I know what you could do." She suggested. "You remember when you spoke to me about one day opening a business that you can one day invest of your own? You're already a financial advisor with your degree in business management and finance, I think you should follow your dreams by opening your very own bank. A bank in your name."

"And I agree." I said. "I'll open up the bank and have it built in the same building of your very own medical practice. We'll make health insurance affordable for everybody."

"You'd really do that for me, True?" She inquired.

"I love you, Zonnique. I'll do anything to make sure you and Zion happy."

I gave her a kiss before making my way inside of the building; getting onto the elevator with a box to pack up my things in the office. As I got off, of the elevator, I was surprised to see a detective leaning on my office door, while smoking a cigarette.

"You must be True Blackwell. I'm looking for your stepbrother Serpent, also known as Snake. I stopped by his apartment, but he wasn't there. Have you happened to see him?" He asked, flicking the cigarette on the floor before stepping on it.

"I haven't seen him." I responded. I thought it was funny the way this word called karma worked. No matter how far you tried to run, one thing about karma, it would always catch up to you.

"Well, if and, when you do see him, tell him I need him to come down to the station. Make sure you pass along the message." The detective said while humming a tune as he walked away.

I entered my office and noticed a sealed envelope under Cyrus's urn. I opened the envelope, unfolding the letter to see a key taped at the top of the paper, with some directions to an unknown destination at the bottom of it. I had a feeling Miss. Fiona was the one who'd left the envelope there. She was the only one who had a key to every room in the office building. When I finished clearing everything out of my office, I picked the box up and got back into the helicopter.

"Is everything okay?" Zonnique asked.

"Everything's straight. We just have to make another stop." I told her while following the directions from the letter and flying to the destination.

When I realized that I was in front of a private bank, I got out and walked up to the teller where I handed him the key.

"Right this way, sir." The teller said, escorting me to the back of the open vault.

He used the key to unlock Cyrus's deposit box and left me to my lonesome. I took out a paper check and stared at it in disbelief. It was a million-dollar college trust fund, signed to his only grandson, Zion McKinney. To be honest, I thought it was one of the best things Cyrus could have ever left in his memory.

"Where to next?" Zonnique asked me.

"Home." I said.

Draped down in a ball gown with my hair pinned in the finest jewels, there was no doubt in my mind about marrying True. As I stood in front of the floor to ceiling mirror, I was in shock that in less than five minutes, I would soon be Mrs. Blackwell.

With shaky hands, I opened the letter that True had written to me for our wedding day.

To my beautiful bride,

I have never been more, sure of anything in my life more than now. I want to commit my heart to you. I want to commit my love to you. I didn't understand what it truly meant to love someone until I met you. You and Zion were always the missing piece to my puzzle, and now that my life is complete, I want to thank you. Thank you for showing me how to chase my dreams in life, thank you for accepting me for me. Thank you for loving me. I can't wait for our wedding night in Paris, so we can start working on our love child. You are my everything and today is the day, I can finally call you my wife.

-LOVE TRUE

A knock on the door of the dressing room caused me to pat my face dry, tucking True's letter into the depth of my breast, right next to my heart.

"I hope I'm not interrupting." Mama Joyce came inside of the room, greeting me with a hug. "I wish I could stay, but it'll be too hard to watch; with Serpent being in jail and all."

"I understand and I'm happy that you at least stopped by." I replied. I was glad that me and Mama Joyce was on good terms, despite the relationship that ended between Serpent and, I.

After Serpent went on Facebook live confessing to the murder of Cyrus, he was found staked out at his mother's house, where he was arrested and charged with his stepfather's murder. I forgave him for beating me, but I felt that it would be better if I kept my distance from him. I didn't wish him any harm, I only hope that as he sat in jail, he took that time to think about what he'd done. I would never take him away from his son; Mama Joyce had my permission to take Zion with her to Serpent's visitations.

"I almost forgot," Mama Joyce said with a smile. "I got Zion a gift for Christmas, something he can always remember his father by." She unzipped this rolling suitcase where a giant snake slithered it's head out.

"Ahhhhh!" I jumped on the counter of the dressing room. "Put it up! Put it up! Mama Joyce, put that damn snake up!"

"Very well then. Maybe when he gets a little bit older."

"Are you ready, baby? Everyone is waiting on you." My mama informed, peeking her head into the dressing room.

As the grand doors in the lobby of the mansion opened, crowds of people stood on their feet. Angels hung down from the ceiling while running their fingers along gold harps. With my mother and father on each side of me, I felt like a queen who was about to meet her king at the throne. As I made it down the aisle, my mother kissed me on my cheek, followed by my father who gave me away. I handed my bouquet to Myrah, who stood behind me with Brooke, as my bridesmaids.

"You may now kiss the bride!" were the words I could hear, as the veil was being lifted from my face. True was crying and so was Zion, who was standing next to him as his best man.

"Didn't I tell you that my heart is true?" True whispered in my ear, before kissing me passionately.

With True holding on to my hand, I laid back on the medical table as the prenatal technician pressed the probe against my growing belly.

"Congratulations Mr. and Mrs. Blackwell! You're exactly thirty-five weeks and should be ready to pop any day now." The technician said as I gazed back at the sonogram screen.

I had been holding twins in my belly and didn't know how they were able to be so active with little to no room left in my stomach.

"Oh, my goodness! I still can't believe we're going to be having twin girls." I cheered as True leaned over, wiping my tears and kissing me on my lips.

"We've been waiting for them to make their arrival and now the day is almost here. Just know that I'm going to be the best husband and father that I can be to our family." True said while Zion came towards my bedside, holding my other hand as he looked over me.

"Are you excited to be a big brother?" I asked Zion.

"Yes, but I'm ready for them to come out," He said while placing his ear on my belly, trying to listen for any movement.

"Have you all thought of any names yet?" The technician asked while taking off her gloves.

We all turned to Zion, who then shouted proudly, "I'm naming my twin sister's Zhuri and Truth!"

The End….

WANT TO INTERACT WITH T'ANN MARIE & HER TEAM? JOIN OUR READERS GROUP ON FACEBOOK @ T'ANN MARIE PRESENTS: THE HOUSE OF URBAN LITERACY! WIN PRIZES, BE APART OF LIVE BOOK DISCUSSIONS & MORE!